FLAW AND ORDER

David and Lisa Barnhardt

NIAGARA PUBLICATIONS

FLAW AND ORDER

By David and Lisa Barnhardt

ISBN 1-56541-001-7

The characters and events described in this book are entirely fictional.

Front cover: reproduction of original oil painting by Ken Brauner, Eugene, Oregon

Cover designed and printed by Ruby Printing, Fair Haven, Vermont

Copyright ©1992 by David and Lisa Barnhardt
All rights reserved under International and Pan-American Copyright Conventions.

Published by Niagara Publications
35960 N. Santiam Highway Gates, OR 97346
Phone (503) 897-2675

Printed in the United States Of America

1

An anemic-looking cat sidled off the porch as Forest Ranger Warren Ascott slammed the pickup door behind him. The fickle March sun was now showing itself, but the Lewis garden remained in shadow, the grass still brown from winter cold. One lonely crocus waved its head in the chill breeze, an unconvincing herald of spring. Parked as close as he was to the house, Warren had to tip his head back to take it all in: a certain washed-out grandeur, it's pale reminders of unheeded luxury, the genteel decay. The weather vane atop the highest roof peak, a wolf with a flying tail terminating in a large metal "S," and nose pointed at a similar "N," sagged precariously at one end, as if to indicate that all wind now blew down. The flagstones shifted under Warren's feet as he approached the porch, signalling the spring thaw more persuasively than did the cheerless garden. Alice Lewis swung the door open before he had a chance to pull the old-fashioned bell.

"Come on in, Warren, and thanks for getting here so soon. I didn't expect you yet. It's such a long drive from Campton."

"You caught me at a good time, Alice. There was nothing much brewing at the Ranger Station, and I was getting cabin fever anyway."

Alice escorted her guest to an ancient-looking horsehair sofa, and swiped at it with the palm of her hand. Dust flew.

"Sorry about the mess, Warren. We hadn't got settled in yet when Monty was released, and since then I haven't been able to concentrate on anything for more than about half a minute."

Her calm manner belied the panic Warren knew she must be feeling, and he admired her control. For

1

thirty years she had maintained a quiet dignity while her husband had endured the many indignities of prison. She had gone about her business in the tiny town of Haven, Oregon without excuses or, apparently, self-pity, raising two children and regularly visiting Monty in the state penitentiary. Warren had met her some ten years earlier, long after Monty Lewis had been convicted of bank robbery and murder. Alice's stoic acceptance of her poverty, loneliness and disgrace at first had been met in the town with pity, and then eventually with respect.

"Don't apologize, Alice, for heaven's sake. Forget the furniture and tell me about Monty. When did you last see him? Why did he take off?"

"Oh, Warren, I can't believe Monty did 'take off,' like you and everyone think. The police haven't taken it seriously at all -- they just figure he did time for murder, he'd do anything. But he wouldn't, Warren. He didn't rob the bank, he didn't kill anybody. And he didn't leave of his own free will without a word to me. He wouldn't do that."

Warren stirred uneasily on the horsehair sofa, sending up another cloud of dust. A quiet sneeze from below made him glance down, and he saw another cat, a tiger, as indolent as the first. Alice gave the cat a push, not overly gentle, with her foot, but succeeded only in scooting him a few inches to the side. The cat favored her with a cool, appraising stare, but didn't move. The silence was becoming awkward. Finally Alice took the bull by the horns.

"You think he's guilty too, don't you, Warren." She said it quietly, without harshness or blame.

"Believe you me, Alice, I never could believe it of Monty -- never could. But ..."

Alice waited wordlessly. She stared out the once-fine bay window into the garden, seeing nothing.

2

"The thing is, Alice, the evidence was so, so ... damning. So complete. So perfect. Your faith in Monty does you credit, honest it does. But when you get right down to it, how could it not have been Monty?"

Alice turned her blue eyes, now faded like the house around her, onto Monty. "I don't know how, Warren. I just know it wasn't. And now he's disappeared and I want him back. Will you help?"

Warren felt somehow rebuked. "Of course I'll help you, Alice, if I can. But what do you expect me to do?"

"You can start by reading this." She handed Warren a bulky, leather-bound book, fastened shut with a leather strap. Dust hid in the crevices of the textured covers. Alice leaned forward and snapped open the book, then leafed through pages, reading upside-down as Warren held the heavy volume. Quickly she found the desired page, and motioned for Warren to read.

"A diary?" Warren was plainly surprised. "I wouldn't have expected Monty to keep a diary."

"He called it his journal. He started it just before Roosevelt was elected. Monty was a worrier, Warren. Sometimes he thought we might never get out of the depression, never have a normal life again; but he wanted the kids to know what a normal life was like. So he'd write down the way things were at the time, compared to how they used to be earlier, before the Depression, thinking he could at least tell them about it, even if he couldn't give it to them. Of course, he never really got the chance ..."

For the first time, Warren understood what a tragically long time thirty years was. The last thirty years had brought him prosperity and happiness in moderation. They had brought poor Monty deprivation and -- and, what? callousness? hatred? -- and to Alice loss and loneliness. Their children had grown up while Monty was in prison. There was no way for Alice to tell them what it was like to grow old, to see your grandchildren, to look back over an expanse of time. With all the accomplishments of human knowledge -- these were the thoughts running through Warren's mind as he looked at Alice -- with all those, there's still so much that we simply couldn't communicate. How to convey our feelings, so rooted in our animal core? Even if they could be exactly recorded or described, the reception of them would still be faulty. The gap between thinking and feeling was too great. Warren's heart ached for Alice at that moment, but he couldn't begin to tell her that.

"Alice, once in a while I come past here, and sometimes I see you standing in the front door, looking out at something. What are you looking at?" he asked curiously.

It took a minute for Alice to respond, as if the words had had to travel a long distance to reach her.

"I'm just looking, Warren." She smiled for the first time that day. "Just looking." Then she became brisk and recalled Warren's attention to the journal. "You should read it all from 1934 on, I think. It won't take long. Monty didn't take it to prison with him, so there's only a few pages after '34. Look at the most recent entry."

Warren obediently read the page Alice had selected. It was dated March 12, 1964.

"Just three days ago? And when did you last see him, Alice?"

"Two days ago. There has to be some connection with this, Warren. Read it!"

He's back. It's been thirty years but that's the face I'll never forget. Now it's my turn.

In spite of himself, Warren was impressed. "I don't suppose you know ..."

"I haven't got the faintest. All I know is that ever since Monty got out of prison two weeks ago, he's thought of nothing but finding out the truth about the robbery and clearing his name. He was determined to do that, come hell or high water. I wanted to put it behind us, you know, try and build a life again. I thought sure the grandkids -- you know Josh and Mary each have two kids of their own now -- anyway, I thought sure Monty wouldn't want to do anything but play with them, build things for them, you know, the usual stuff. Was I ever wrong! Oh, Warren, he was just obsessed with what happened thirty years ago, with ancient history as far as I'm concerned. He didn't take an interest in this big old house I bought last fall, or the kids or grandkids, not even me, really. Just in passing, you know, like he had the feelings of a ghost and not a man; I mean, the same feelings he always had, but so washed-out, like. I'm putting it all wrong, but now he's gone altogether, and I know he wouldn't leave me to worry if he could help it. Something's wrong in a very big way, Warren. I'm positive."

Warren nodded. "I believe you, Alice. You say Monty was obsessed with all this. What exactly was he doing these last couple weeks? How did he spend his time?"

"He spent most of it rooting through old boxes and trunks until he found that journal. Then he started spending his days at libraries."

"Libraries? Doing research or something?"

"I'm not sure. I think he was reading newspapers, judging by the smudges on his hands and face when he'd come home. I'd guess old newspapers, from thirty years ago. You could probably find out for sure

5

from the librarians. They're bound to remember him. His release was a big deal around here, you know. It got him his pictures in all the papers again."

"Would that be the Milford Public Library?"

"I think so. Also once or twice he may have gone into Salem, to the state library. I'm not just sure."

Warren negotiated his long frame out of the broken-down sofa, and heard another sneeze from the cat. He hated to leave Alice on such a dreary note.

"This is quite a house. How did you ever come by it?"

Alice smiled again, a bit ruefully, Warren thought.

"I thought we needed a fresh start, what with having Monty home again and all. There didn't seem to be much in our price range, especially old mansions like this. It was built before the turn of the century, you know. But this was dirt cheap. I guess it must need more work than the real estate agent let on about, but I figured even that was good -- it would give Monty and me something to do. So I took the plunge, sold our other house, and here we are."

"Well, as long as the foundation and roof are good, you're set," said Warren, relying on a conversation he had overheard in the hardware store some time back.

"Just find Monty for me, Warren, and I'll be set for life."

Warren gave her a quick hug and made his way back over the shifting flagstones, Monty's journal under his arm.

2

August 1933

A solitary prospector crossing the mile-high ridge that separated the Chinook River Valley from the Yellow Creek drainage basin, was leaning with his back against a lone tree. He was taking one last look at the Chinook River four thousand feet below him. As he absently scratched his dark beard, the prospector noticed that the river's course seemed more like a silver thread than the hurly-burly current it was. The slopes on either side of the narrow valley into which he was gazing were covered with beautiful stands of mature Douglas fir and hemlock trees in an infinite, wavering hue of green. The old man's sharp eyesight enabled him to discern the town of Linnton on the riverbanks about sixteen miles downstream. Directly below him was the busy but small town of Milford, from which he had departed about two hours earlier. Upstream he could trace the river another three miles to the tiny canyon that cradled Haven. This was the last town on the river for many more miles upstream into the mountains. By shading his eyes against the sun the observer could barely make out the old wagon road, tracking the river where possible, from Haven down to Linnton, where it disappeared in the haze on its way to Salem.

On this stretch of river a new element had appeared and progressed steadily in the last year. The railroad now reached from Salem clear out to Haven, still seventy miles short of its target terminus across the Cascade Range. When finished, the railroad would provide a means of transporting the products of the Willamette Valley to Chicago-bound trains and the markets of the eastern United States. The prospector could see the cut of the railroad through the timber much more clearly than he could see the wagon road, which was crossed several times by the more direct line of the railroad. He could see activity as the men, horses and mules struggled to build the track, but couldn't make out the construction workers themselves.

Rested, the prospector reluctantly arose, grunted as he replaced the pack on his broad shoulders, and resumed his trip to the gold claims of Yellow Creek.

As the work engine blew the end of lunch break, the construction crew visible from far above resumed its labors. The conglomeration of Englishmen, Swedes, Bulgarians, Chinese and other assorted people was racing time and the depletion of investors' money to push the railroad over the Cascades. Every sleepy little town they reached along the line was suddenly inundated by the bustling crowd of railroad builders.

Gil Callahan was the entrepreneurial free spirit behind the new railroad line, and he had a talent for locating potential investors. Nonetheless, progress had been slower than anticipated, due mainly to heavy rains. Small streams would suddenly become raging torrents and wipe out trestles and small bridges overnight. The tracks already reached beyond Milford and were producing a modest profit, thanks in large part to Tobe Tobias and his Milford sawmill, one of the largest in the west and a major customer of the railroad. Abner Brillo, owner of the bank in Milford, also benefitted from the wealth represented by the railroad. The main financial goal of the construction would not be attained, however, unless the track could be completed another seventy miles to Bend. The reward for reaching Bend would be grants by the federal government of every alternate section of land for a width of two miles for the entire length of the railroad, from Milford to Bend. The land not yet breached by the railroad contained some of the finest timber in the United States. Although not yet worth much, it would some day make a baron of the enterprising builder or financier who could anticipate the needs of the future.

What no one anticipated was the blood to be spilled along the way.

The prospector continued on his solitary way, savoring his independence from the swarm below.

* * *

In the small town of Haven, 1934 opened with gently falling snow, the flakes as large as silver dollars. This continued off and on every day until early February, when it suddenly stopped and left nearly four feet of snow behind it. Men and boys and some women were busily shoveling roofs. Even the train was not able to get through for five weeks. That part was not unusual in the winter, nor overly bothersome, since the train was not needed for hauling logs this time of year. Deer were hunted, although now less successfully since taking refuge from the hunters and their dogs in the higher mountain elevations.

On one of these snowy nights, Monty Lewis and his family crawled into their beds a little earlier than usual. Monty had been lucky enough to stumble on a small deer, and by the time he had packed it down the mountain through the deep snow he was exhausted.

"Good night, Alice. Bet I beat you to sleep. I'm mighty tired." To his surprise, Alice was already curled up on her side and asleep. He turned out the kerosene lamp and crawled into bed beside her.

Some time later, Monty awoke from an unsettling dream that he could not remember but dimly disliked, and found that he couldn't get back to sleep. He quietly left the bedroom, being careful not to awaken Alice or the children, and searched for a match in the darkness of the living room. When the kerosene lamp flooded one end of the room with a warm light and its accompanying pungent odor, he walked over to the Sears Roebuck battery radio and flipped it on.

That was the latest news of the day. The words that our new president, Franklin Roosevelt, spoke one year ago in his Inaugural Address still ring true today. He stressed trust and hard work, along with patience, for help in dragging us from this awful quagmire of economic depression. He ended his plea to the country that night with the words: "The only thing we have to fear is fear itself." Thank you and goodnight.

Impatiently Monty switched off the radio.

"Easy for him to say," he muttered.

Although Monty, like Roosevelt, truly believed that things would get better, he couldn't shed the anxiety that had become his constant companion. The worries about warm clothes for the kids, about the future, even about food, never left Monty, and he felt as never before the burden of being a family man. Instead of returning to the bedroom, Monty withdrew his journal from the bureau drawer and began writing.

January 12, 1934. The wishbook really came through for us this Christmas. There's no way we could have got into town in this snow to the general store; and anyway, I'd be embarrassed buying presents for the kids there with my debt to Oliver what it is. He'd think it pretty funny me plunking down hard cash for ribbons and a Tonka truck, when I ask him for credit every month to get salt pork and coffee. No need for anybody to know that I hocked my beaver traps to buy presents for the kids and Alice. Enough left to see us through another few months, too. Not like when I was a kid, though, no sir. Dad had presents for everybody, and all on the salary of schoolteacher. Back then you didn't have to ask old Ollie, or anybody, to wait another week or two on the bill, or watch your wife cut up flour sacks to make shirts for the kids -- though by God when she's finished you'd never know they was once flour sacks. I guess it could be worse. What with the venison and grouse and the huckleberries and blackcaps Alice has canned, we're alot better off than most folks. Anyway, thank God for the Sears & Roebuck wishbook, and for kids who think a penny's worth of trinkets is a big deal. I just hope to hell I can figure out some way to get us through when the trap money runs out. Alice says I worry too much. Maybe so, but she's not the one who has to do the figuring.

Monty put the journal aside and decided he was sleepy again. Before climbing back into bed, he drew back the window curtains and attempted to peer outside in the dark to see if it was snowing again; but the snow sliding off the roof and the four feet of it on the ground had combined to completely cover the window.

"Damn," he murmured, "we'll have to shovel some more in the morning to get to the outhouse."

It was almost daylight when Monty awoke and stumbled from bed in his nightshirt on his way to stoke up the wood stove.

"Check on the kids and see if they're okay," whispered Alice.

Monty tried to be quiet as he opened the stove damper and put a couple of fir chunks in the stove. Peeking into the children's bedroom he could see Josh covered to the chin in his trundle bed, and Mary in hers but with the covers kicked off. Monty quietly replaced them and stood studying the children for a few moments. Josh's freckles were more noticeable in the mornings, as was Mary's blonde hair. It hardly seemed possible that Josh was seven and Mary five already. It might have been only yesterday that he and Alice had talked of marriage for the first time on a cold snowy night eight years ago while cuddled up in his dad's Model T Ford.

Returning to his own room, he discovered that Alice was up and restoring a semblance of normality to the bed covers.

"My, you look pretty this early in the morning," he remarked.

"I'd look a whole lot prettier, Mister, if I had something other than this old holey flannel nightgown to sleep in."

"Well, maybe I can do something about that, Ma'am."

"Talk is cheap."

Monty walked over to her side of the bed. Just then a sound of giggling startled Alice.

"Mary, you get back to bed this instant. How long have you been standing there?"

"Oh, just a few minutes, Mommy. You and Daddy look funny in the morning."

"Well, you scamper back to bed, young lady. It's a little early yet." Mary returned to her own room and found that Josh was awake, too.

"Where have you been?" he demanded to know.

Mary gave a sniff of superiority and settled down into her still-warm bed. "None of your business."

"Hmph. Who cares, anyway! You and your Big Secrets." And Josh pulled the covers up over his nose and went back to sleep.

3

The winter wore on, and its high points were duly recorded by Monty Lewis in his journal. The monotony of March was broken by a small celebration in the Lewis family.

> Today was Alice's birthday. I wanted to give her that hat she's been admiring at the dry goods store in Linnton, but couldn't afford it. Surprise, surprise. But I think this was even better. I recaned the seats of old man Crossburn's wicker chairs, and talked him into giving me first pick of his trapline in return. And I'll be damned if he didn't catch a mink in one instead of a muskrat! So I latched onto that mink, cleaned it and tanned it and gave it to Alice first thing this morning. Oh, lordy, was she ever tickled. Said she'd make some earmuffs for Mary from it, but I put my foot down and said it had to be something for her, not the kids or me or anybody else. Well, she liked that alright, deep down, and said after all she could use a muff, and wouldn't that just make the finest muff you ever saw? I told her how I came by it. I know she thinks I should have got some lumber out of Crossburn, seeing as how he's assistant manager at the saw mill and I got to get the springhouse fixed up before it falls to pieces under the next snow. But I'll be damned if my wife goes without on her birthday. Anyhow, she didn't say a word about that, just hugged me and told me how

she could always count on me to come through.

Otherwise, the days brought their usual contingent of restrained pleasures and family squabbles. On Sundays Alice set out an especially hearty morning meal.

"Come and get it before I throw it to the dog," she shouted out the kitchen window to her two children, who had managed to build the better part of a snow fort before breakfast, getting themselves thoroughly soaked in the process.

Mary shouted back. "You wouldn't do that, Mommy, would you?"

Alice reminded herself that Mary took things very literally, and smiled as she recalled how frightened her daughter had been upon hearing that, due to a late payment on a short-term loan, Abner Brillo had jumped down Monty's throat. Mary had inquired anxiously whether Dad would have to go see Doc Golden. Alice's reminiscences were cut short by a childish howl from outside. She stepped quickly to the back door.

"What are you up to out here?" she demanded sternly.

Wailing loudly, Mary was brushing snow from her face and pointing accusingly at Josh. "He told me to!"

Transferring her gaze to her son while wiping Mary's tears away, Alice said merely, "Well?"

Chortling in satisfaction, Josh responded, "I didn't think she'd really do it! Who'd of guessed she'd fall for it?"

Mary interposed heatedly, "You told me to! You said it was a scientific speriment!"

"That's it," said Alice firmly. "Mary, tell me what happened."

Grudgingly, the young one responded. "Josh said they were studying gravity at school, and to see how far I could lean forward."

"So?" Alice prompted impatiently.

Josh couldn't resist, and added triumphantly, "With her hands in her pockets!"

Still sniffling, Mary complained, "I fell right on my nose! It hurt and it still hurts. I think it's broken."

"Josh, shame on you. Now, honey," Alice turned to Mary. "It isn't broken. It isn't even bleeding. But," she added severely to Josh, "it certainly might have been. You have no business pulling tricks like that on your sister. There'll be no dessert for you after dinner."

"Aw, Mom, she was in the snow when she fell. She couldn't a got hurt for real."

"That's enough, Josh. Now, both of you get inside and into dry clothes. Breakfast is waiting. And close that door behind you! Were you born in a barn?"

Finally, Monty and the children sat down to a wintertime breakfast of pancakes topped with blackberry jam in place of syrup, and fried eggs.

"The eggs are runny, Mom," Mary said reproachfully.

Before Alice could respond, Josh observed, "Hey, my socks are different colors. Mom, could you get me another black one?"

Turning to his son, Monty interjected, "Are your legs broken? Go get it yourself. Mom hasn't even had a chance to sit down and eat yet."

Rubbing her nose tentatively, Mary noted, "It hurts. I think it really is broken."

"Say, Dad," Josh said, ignoring Mary and forgetting about his socks, "we're studying rodents in school. Did you know that gerbils eat their young?"

Alice turned from the stove and gazed at her offspring. "Is that a fact?" she murmured speculatively.

Laughing, Monty warned, "You didn't pick the best time to go putting ideas in your Mom's head, Josh. Now run and get that sock."

At last Alice sat down at the table with her own breakfast. "Monty, that roof on the springhouse is about to go. I'm not sure it'll last out the winter." The Lewises were lucky enough to have a spring so close by that the springhouse was connected to the main house. Year round it provided excellent water, and in the summer served as cool storage as well, for the many preserves and other products that couldn't stand heat.

"Sure, Honey. I said I'd take care of it."

Alice smiled at him. "I dimly remember you saying that, alright. Two years ago you said it."

"And I meant it! I just didn't say when." Monty returned the smile.

"Also, I need some more wood split for the cook stove first thing today."

"I know, Alice, but first I'll have to shovel the snow out of the way before I can get into the wood shed. We've had lots more snow these last two winters than what we were having before. It's like we're living smack up in the mountains instead of here in the valley."

Like many communities in the area, Haven was around a thousand feet above sea level. Higher in the mountains the winters were colder and the summers shorter. Haven's mildness in climate was paid for by getting in the form of rain the moisture that higher landed as snow, but the air still held the mountain purity. Most families in Haven and neighboring towns had their own gardens and fruit trees. Blackberries from back east had been transplanted to the valleys of this country, and now were flourishing even if left to the wild. Much canning was done, for most families ate more as the snow reached greater depths. Wild huckleberries grew high up on the mountains where a forest fire had cleared out some of the fir and hemlock timber, giving the berries breathing room.

After Monty had the woodbox full he carried in half a deer from the woodshed where it had been hung to cool out. He commenced butchering the venison so that Alice could get it canned. Later, as he was outside feeding the scrap meat and bones to his brown and white mongrel dog, he noticed some cougar tracks in the snow.

"So that's what you were barking about last night! What's the matter, Chief, didn't you want to take him on by yourself?" He gave the dog an affectionate pat. Chief promptly returned to his eating or, more precisely, his gobbling.

After stomping the snow from himself at the back door Monty remarked to Alice, who was busily cramming venison into Mason jars, "I found fresh cougar tracks behind the woodshed. Might be a chance to get a fifty-dollar bounty if we could tree him."

Alice paused in her canning. "It sure would come in handy. You won't be able to work in the woods again until at least May and, as deep as the snow is this winter, maybe even June. Our grocery bill at Toonan's will be sky high."

"Yeah, I know," Monty sighed, "but with all this stuff you've canned and pickled and preserved and a little free meat now and then, we can probably hold out till spring."

He slipped into his corked boots and donned a heavily-lined denim jacket and a wool stocking cap for the attempt to track down the cougar. When Josh saw the preparations he pleaded to go, but to no avail.

"No, Josh, that snow is deeper than you are tall. You're a little too young yet "

"But Dad! I'm seven!"

Monty was not persuaded, and set off on his own. After breaking trail down the railroad for a few hundred yards, he knocked at the shack of Barney Pritchart. Barney was a forty-year-old bachelor, and related in some complicated fashion to Abner Brillo, who owned the local bank.

"Come on in," roared a voice from inside. "What's up, Monty?"

As Monty surveyed the dingy interior of the one-room cabin, Barney was pouring him a tumblerful of moonshine whiskey. "Here, have a snort of this to wet your whistle. Straight from Gabe Hanks to you."

Already acquainted with the quality of whiskey produced by the local distiller, Monty declined the drink and explained about the cougar tracks. "Just wondered if you wanted to bring your two hounds, and if we get this varmint we split the bounty."

"Sounds good to me, Monty. Let's go." Most things did sound good to Barney Pritchart, who was easily amused and not terribly selective about his entertainment. His attention span was short and his interests varied: a little whiskey, a little hunting and trapping, and a little -- very little -- steady work. Recently Pritchart had been hired on at the bank as a teller, a piece of good fortune which most people attributed to his family ties with the Brillos. Barney's partially-bald head and sometimes shaky hands made him seem closer to sixty than his actual forty years.

It didn't take long to get the yapping hounds on the cougar's trail, which headed due north toward the mountains. The frozen crust of the snow was substantial enough to carry the dogs' weight, but Monty and Barney soon found themselves floundering waist deep in it. By this time the hounds were out of sight and even their baying was growing faint.

"We can't hack this, Barney. We'll have to head for home. But what about the dogs?"

"Don't worry. They'll come home in a day or two. You can't get them lost around here."

By noon Barney and Monty were back in Haven. When they walked in the house Alice asked, "Back already? I figured that cougar might run the dogs all day."

"No such luck." Monty explained the shortened trip to Alice. "Is it alright for Barney to stay for lunch?"

"You know it is, silly. That is, if Mr. Pritchart can eat my cooking."

Pritchart looked appreciatively at the lived-in appearance of the home. "This house sure looks more comfortable than before you folks moved in. Back then the walls were still covered with burlap. Now you got wallpaper on the walls and print linoleum on the floors."

"I'd have to thank Alice and her dad, Gus Swetzer, for most of the improvements. They did a terrific job. About the only thing I need to change now is to get rid of the ivy from the outside walls. It tries to pull that old plank siding right off the house."

"Your fruit trees have sure grown," said Pritchart. "Reminds me of the ones Art Crossburn planted around that fancy house of his. When did he build that house, anyway?"

"Let me think. Must have been about 1925 when he was hired on as sawmill manager by old man Tobias."

Alice interjected, "He didn't actually build it, though, he just added on to what was already there. Made it alot grander."

Pritchart remarked, "Art Crossburn sure had a streak of bad luck since he moved in there."

"Are you boys ready to eat?" said Alice. "You can continue your weighty talk after lunch. What would you like for dessert, Barney?"

"Anything, as long as it's canned huckleberries," he said promptly.

Lunch consisted of fresh venison, gravy and biscuits fresh out of the oven, followed by the huckleberries Barney had requested.

"Care for another cup of coffee, Barney?"

As Monty poured a second cup he returned to the topic of the Crossburns. "Art's wife died about five years ago, didn't she?"

"Yes," answered Pritchart, as he mopped up the last of his gravy with half a biscuit, "and two years after that his oldest daughter was taken to the funny farm in Salem."

Alice chimed in. "Have you noticed the cough Art's developed this winter? It's one thing after another with the poor fellow." She added philosophically, "When it rains it pours."

A silence of contentment followed the satisfying meal. Eventually Monty said, "That talk about Art reminds me of something I wanted to tell you, Alice. Barney here mentioned that the sawmill in Milford has some openings on swingshift, and I'm going to try and get on there. It would mean working from four in the afternoon to midnight, but it beats a kick in the rear with a frosty boot. It would just be until spring, when the logging opens up. We need some cash money mighty bad."

"You must need it if you're willing to pull on that green chain in the mill -- I know and Alice knows you hate it and you'd have to be looking at Tobias's ugly face every day." This from Pritchart, who took a dim view of any work.

"You're dead right, but I can stand anything for a month or two ..."

Alice interrupted. "See if you can get my brother Richard on. He can use the work, too."

"I know Richard needs a job, but does the job need him?" Monty became more diplomatic when he saw Alice's eyes narrowing. "Okay, I'll try my best, but he sure wore out his welcome with most of the folks around here."

A knock on the door interrupted their talk. Monty opened it to find Abner Brillo on the porch. "Well, this is a surprise. Come in, Abner."

The visitor stepped inside and said brusquely, "I'm looking for Barney Pritchart. His shack is empty, but I noticed the trail in the snow between your place and his, and thought maybe I'd catch him here."

Nodding, Monty responded, "You've come to the right place. Go on in the kitchen, that's where you'll find him."

"Thanks, Monty," said Abner, "but if it's all the same to you, I'd just as soon see him outside." And he stepped back out on the porch, scowling.

"Hmp. Have it your way." Monty conveyed the message to Barney, who thanked Alice for the lunch, picked up his coat and left.

"What was that all about?" Alice inquired of her husband.

Shrugging, Monty replied, "Beats me. Judging by the temper Brillo was in, I'd guess there's trouble at the bank."

4

By the first of April the snow had mostly disappeared from Haven. Richard Swetzer stopped at Monty's house in a borrowed Model T Ford, and honked the horn rather impatiently.

"Come on, Monty," he shouted, "Milford and our future await."

Inside the house Alice spoke tartly. "What's that racket all about, Monty, and what's this about your future waiting in Milford?"

"You know, today's the trip to get work at the sawmill. As you can see, or hear, I should say, your brother Richard is going in with me."

As Monty kissed Alice goodbye she murmured, "Good luck."

"We'll need it with a cast of two like us going to audition!"

Monty climbed in beside his brother-in-law and they left Haven not in a cloud of dust, but in a whirl of backfiring and muddy water. The road to Haven was referred to as a gravelled road, but at this time of year cars almost needed chains to get through. At least they didn't have to worry about getting hit by a train as the road crossed and recrossed the train tracks seven times during the four miles to Milford; the train would not start hauling logs from the upper canyon timber until all the snow had melted, probably around the first of May.

Richard Swetzer was a well-built man of thirty-five. His ready smile and smoothly-combed hair topped the figure of a man in motion. Unfortunately, bootleg whiskey purchased from Gabe Hanks was his downfall. He tried to get by on a smile and ready wit instead of hard work, which meant jumping from job to job. Monty had a hard time believing that Richard was actually related to his Alice.

The new board sidewalks in Milford soon appeared as the two men neared the mill office. Tobe Tobias's sawmill spread on both sides of the river and dominated the heart of Milford. It employed about three hundred and fifty men, and even a few women were now working on some of the chains used to transport the heavy sheets of wood through processing. It was considered the largest sawmill in the United States as the winter of 1934 melted into spring.

"Hello, men. If you're looking for work you've picked the right day. We need about eight more yet for swing shift." This from Tom Rice, combination hiring boss and paymaster, addressing the small group of men who showed up regularly on the off-chance of finding work.

Richard Swetzer spoke up quickly. "No days open?"

"Nope. 'Fraid not," answered Rice. "This is all we have. Take it or leave it."

"We'll take it," Monty said glumly, "but I'm not sure how long I'll stand it. I guess your money is as good as anybody's, though."

"Okay. Since I know all of you, here's ten dollars of company script you can spend in our store. That should help until payday. Be here at four o'clock tomorrow with a pair of gloves. Sign here for the script."

Before they could do as requested, Tobe Tobias strode into the room, slamming the door behind him. At almost six feet three inches tall and with a shock of flaming red hair, Tobe was a striking individual who was prone to get his way regardless of whom it might hurt. He was a hard drinker and gambler, a success with women, and the owner of the largest

23

sawmill and logging operation in Oregon. When the timber market was solid and everyone eager to build in the boom of the 1920s, he was the king pin of the area. The Depression slowed him down, but did not wound him mortally. He lived in Milford but spent much time in his various logging camps in the area, especially Camp Eighteen up Blowout Creek, where over half his timber was logged in the mid-1930s. He continually earned his reputation as a son of a bitch.

"Rice, you blundering idiot! What the hell are you still signing men up for?" the boss demanded.

Taken aback, the paymaster began justifying himself. "Well, you know, we still haven't filled the swing shift. We could use more manpower." He gestured to Richard and Monty. "Like them."

"Get with it, Rice. We have all the workers we need." Tobias grinned. "I just shipped in a whole load of Japs. They work for half what these local boys want, and do twice the work. They show up on time because they don't go out hellin' around after work, makin' old Hanks rich by buyin' that poison of his." He paused and looked Monty and Richard up and down. "And that's Swetzer, isn't it? It'd be a cold day in hell before I'd hire him, Japs or no Japs." So saying, the mill owner reached forward and snatched the script back from both of them. "Better luck next time, boys," he said, and turned on his heel and left.

Mortified, Tom Rice shook his head but said nothing.

Also silent, Monty grabbed Richard by the arm and led him out of the office, ignoring his protests and oaths.

As they dodged mud holes on the walk back to the car, Monty flushed with anger as he replayed in his mind the scene with Tobias. Richard continued to fume.

"And the way he grabbed that script back! Like we were gonna run off with it or something! Of all the lousy, worthless --"

"Forget it, Richard. No sense letting him get you down."

"Get me down! As if he could. It's just that God-awful, high-falutin', holier-than-thou attitude of his that burns me up. Local men aren't good enough, anymore, huh? How does he think he got where he is?" Richard continued talking, half to himself, in the car. To divert him, Monty made a suggestion.

"How 'bout a drink, Richard?"

As Monty had expected, this idea was greeted enthusiastically, and they were soon seated in the tavern.

Milford's business district was one block long. On the west side was Brillo's bank, next to it the tavern, then Albert Toonan's grocery -- all one story wooden false fronts except the bank, which had been faced with red brick. Across the street was a three-story wood-sided boarding house with a restaurant on part of the first floor. Next to it was a drug store with its inevitable soda fountain and ice cream counter. A barbershop and clothing/variety store filled the last of the block. Around the corner from the bank was a short street called Wall Street along the railroad. The only buildings on this street were the small depot and express office for the railroad, and also the hospital. Almost any need of the valley people could be found in one of these stores, including quite an assortment of liquor. The normal population of Milford was seven hundred and sixty.

Afternoons were usually busy at the Milford Tavern, and this day was no exception.

"Hi Richard! Come on over and pull up a couple of chairs." The invitation was from Gabe Hanks, who spent most of his time in Milford and the rest at a small cabin he had recently built below Coffin Mountain. "Big John and I were just discussing those Japs old man Tobias has been hiring for his mill."

"That's a pretty sore subject with us," remarked Monty, and he proceeded to describe their reception at the sawmill.

"Hey, barkeep, how about a couple beers for these guys. Sounds like they could use it."

"Thanks, John," said Richard as he sank down in the chair. "Bring me a double shot along with that."

As they relaxed in the warm room John commented, "Yeah, Tobe has gone and hired some Japanese to work in the sawmill and he's been laying off local men to make room for them."

Gabe chimed in, "They work for half what the local hands do. Shows you what that Tobe will do for a dollar." Gabe said it bitterly, for the men laid off were good customers for his moonshine, while the Japanese didn't waste any of their money on it.

John intoned, "I was hoping to get hired on again, but now I can see I never will if this keeps up. All they do is steal our jobs and eat and sleep in that big house they rented behind the lodge hall. Never do nothin' but work and sleep and maybe go to Linnton or Salem on Saturday night."

The bartender brought another round of drinks over. "These are from Gil Callahan," he explained.

"Thanks, Gil," said Gabe sociably. "Come on over and we'll tell you our troubles." Callahan stirred from a corner table and joined them.

"You see, Gil, we've been trying to decide what to do about those Japs taking our jobs. Got any ideas?"

"Blow 'em up," solemnly replied Gil, who had a two-hour head start on his drinking.

"Why not?" Gabe was quick to pick up on this. "A few sticks of dynamite in that house of theirs will get the message across."

"But where will we get dynamite this time of week?" Richard inquired excitedly.

Big John quickly spoke. "No problem. I've got a key to the powder house. And now will be a good time. They should all be on their way to Linnton by now."

There was a general buzz of conversation. Only Callahan demurred.

"Count me out of the action, boys. I can think of 'em, but I'm getting too old to carry out this kind of monkey business." He arose and started walking out. "You coming, Gabe?" Reluctantly, Gabe left, too.

Big John looked across at Richard and Monty. "You two chickening out, too?"

After further discussion of strategy, they both agreed to do it.

That night the quiet of Milford was shattered by sixteen sticks of Hercules dynamite blowing up the large white house directly behind the lodge hall. Every window on the back side of the two-story lodge hall was blown out. The authorities could never discover who had been responsible. The only thing known for certain was that the men who had been laid off from the sawmill were recalled to work the next Tuesday.

Monty recorded the event in his journal.

> It seemed like a good idea at the time, and even afterwards. Hell, it got those men their jobs back -- good men, good jobs. Alice threw a fit when she heard about it. I've got a sneaking suspicion she knows I was in on it, but she didn't say so. She just went on and on about how we're all savages at heart anyway,

and the only thing that keeps us from being animals is controlling our passions, and what not. Made quite a speech about how everybody's alike when they get mean, whether it's a schoolyard bully or a group of drunks acting like -- well, like we were acting; and the only difference is whether you're doing it or getting it done to you. She said ... oh, hell, she said alot and made me feel like a damned gangster. Like if that's all it takes to turn men from a crowd into a mob we shouldn't be allowed out without our mothers. I told her it was frontier justice, and she just laughed at that. But it was frontier justice, which sometimes is the only justice we have here. It wasn't fair, that money going to Japanese. Sometimes you have to take things into your own hands. Still in all, I guess Alice did make me feel like a bully.

5

Alice and her mother, Anna Swetzer, were co-hostesses for the May meeting of the Milford Women's Improvement Club. The subject of the day's meeting was a debate: who has the most influence on a family's children -- the mother or the father? Elizabeth Lewis, Monty's sister, staunchly presented the mother's side, while Mrs. Arnold Golden, the doctor's wife, was prevailed upon to represent the father's side. After an hour of heated debated, Mrs. Golden was voted the winner. The ten or so ladies enjoyed a lunch of home-smoked salmon and cheese washed down with the last of the previous season's cider.

As the ladies finished their good-byes, Alice quickly dressed Josh and Mary in their best clothes. Her father Gus had promised to pick them up on the railroad speeder and take them into Milford for the afternoon. Shortly after one o'clock Josh first heard the clickety-clack of the hand-pumped speeder coming down the rails. His grandfather's muscular arms were pumping the speeder into Haven at a good clip. Gus had his own speeder, and the railroad permitted him to use the rails anytime a train was not scheduled. Alice and the children settled back with pleasure for the trip into Milford. It was a warm May day and the trees were either in bloom or leafing out, and hearts were feeling younger.

By this time spring had melted all the snow in the valley, and most of it higher up in the mountains. The local men, including Monty, were back at work in the woods. Alice had Monty's second paycheck of the season and hoped to cash it at Abner Brillo's bank. The bank was located next to the train depot on the one-block street called Wall Street -- a little touch of Abner's.

Alice enjoyed the ride into town, with the happy chatter of her children in her ears and the air heavy with the perfume of spring. She re-knotted her scarf under her chin as they picked up speed, so as to look presentable and not wind-blown when they arrived. The journey seemed a short one, and once they had coasted into the depot Alice permitted the children to stay there with Gus, so that they could place pennies on the rails in hopes of seeing them flattened by passing trains.

As Alice stepped into the bank she was greeted warmly by Abner. He was a small man with an unruly shock of gray hair framing a smiling face.

"Good morning, Mrs. Lewis. I haven't had a chance to apologize for barging in on you a while back to talk to Barney. Sorry about that."

29

"No need to be, Mr. Brillo. I'm sure you had your reasons," Alice responded graciously but curiously.

The bank owner leaned forward and spoke confidentially. "Between you and me, there was a bit of a problem. The records kept in the normal course of business --"

Just then Barney Pritchart himself emerged from an inner office.

"Speak of the devil," Alice murmured.

Abner broke off his story, and instead thanked Alice loudly for her patronage of the bank. Responding in kind, Alice said good-bye to him and walked up to the teller's window. She presented her check to the bank's only teller, Pete Justin. He was in his late seventies and was perpetually planning to retire.

"Well, I see you're still here, Pete. Got enough money left to cash this?"

"You bet, Mrs. Lewis, plenty. Oh, wait a minute." He scrutinized the check. "Excuse me just a minute, Mrs. Lewis." Justin hurried off and held a brief discussion with Abner Brillo. "Sure, we can cash this. No problem. And by the way, I am going to retire this summer for sure. Yep, made up my mind." He reached into a rack of silver dollars and then finished counting the rest out in greenbacks. "Good morning, Mrs. Lewis."

Alice stopped at Toonan's Grocery. She bought some flour, sugar, bologna, and candy for the kids, and paid some on her bill.

On the way back Gus stopped long enough in Haven for Alice to leave her groceries, then they all rode on to the homestead for a visit with her mother. The homestead had been acquired by Alice's grandparents straight from the American government, free of charge but with strings attached. The Swetzers had to live on the property for seven years before they could get title free and clear. The lure of free, rich land in Oregon was so great to the Swetzers and many other immigrants, especially from northern Europe, that the government's goal of encouraging settlement in this wilderness was easily met.

Gus was proud of the homestead, and Josh and Mary loved it there. There were chickens and cows, even a couple of horses. Anna had a huge wood cookstove which always had a kettle of something good simmering on one corner, and usually a pie in the oven. The kids liked best to go down to the "fish market" with their grandfather when the salmon were running up the river. The fish market was a four-foot falls in the river which required several tries by a jumping salmon to make it over the obstacle. In the meantime Gus could usually spear a few of them for later smoking in the smoke house.

Gus had almost two hundred cords of wood stacked along the train tracks for use by the train in its fuel-consuming boiler. The railroad paid him four dollars a cord, which amounted to quite a bit of cash money for Gus and his family during the year.

Alice and the children walked the mile back to Haven to end what had been a pleasant and fun day. It was so nice to see spring again, with most of the men either back working or making plans for it. As they walked, Alice was momentarily plagued by the anxiety she felt whenever she thought of Monty working in the woods. Dangerous work in itself, the risk was compounded by the attitude of Monty's boss, Tobe Tobias. Rumor had it that the previous summer a young man had been hurt on one of Tobe's jobs, and left to lie in the heat until quitting time so as to avoid losing work-time transporting him to town. The man died that night, and many in the community blamed it on Tobe. When Alice had spoken of her fears to Monty, however, he had merely reassured her about his knowledge of logging. Her husband had conceded the Tobias mean streak and had promised to be careful; then he had folded her in an embrace. Recalling this, Alice pushed her worries aside with an effort of will, and determined to enjoy the remainder of the day as much as she had the rest of it. Sniffing the mountain air appreciatively, with its heady scent of fir needles and violets, Alice felt like a young girl again.

6

The No. 10 Shay steam locomotive chugged its way up Blowout Creek with a snorting of steam and a trail of smoke behind. The narrow-gauge track stayed close to the creek, and even then the grade was steep enough to require a steady stream of four-foot long wood chunks thrown by the fireman into the ravenous boiler. Camp 18 was just a short distance up Blowout Creek from its junction with the Chinook River. Since this was Monday morning the train stopped a few minutes in Camp 18 to unload the cook and some supplies and to pick up the two or three loggers who had chosen to remain in camp over the weekend.

Monty was riding in the camp car at the rear of the train, separated from the steam engine by fourteen empty log cars. Camp 18 had been constructed the previous year, and was new to Monty. One of the men picked up at the camp for transport to the logging site higher up was Joe Harbison, a forty-year veteran of logging but so crippled by many small accidents that he was relegated to the lowly job of whistle punk. His duties consisted mainly of transmitting information to the men all over the logging site by means of coded signals on a steam whistle.

"How are you, young fellow?" Joe grunted as he sat down on the hard bench beside Monty. "My name's Joe Harbison, and what might your'n be?"

"Monty Lewis. I noticed you were staying at camp. What kind of camp is it? Any good?"

"Oh, it's okay. Just the usual big bunkhouses and cook shack. Old Gabe Hanks does run a small bar there when he's not busy delivering moonshine somewhere. Better stay clear of him, though -- he'll steal the shirt off your back one way or t'other."

With a couple short whistle warnings, the Shay lurched forward and each car jerked into motion with a quick bump. Monty looked back as the train rounded a curve. The camp was set in a partial clearing among the fir trees. All the structures were crudely built from rough lumber, yet cleverly designed to be quickly disassembled and loaded on the train for transportation to the next logging site.

The area presently being logged was only four or five miles upstream. Tobe Tobias had hired Gil Callahan to lay the track as the train progressed further upstream. "Hired" was probably the wrong term to use, for actually Callahan was laying the track pursuant to a contract drawn by Tobias.

When the train ground to a stop with its usual hissing of steam, Monty was one of the first to jump off.

"Let's go hunt up the head man, you guys. I think it's Big John who's the bull buck today."

At the end of the rails sat the large railroad yarder. It was a wood-eating monster powered by steam. The height and width allowed the empty train cars to back under and through it. The locomotive's engine, now pulling from the opposite end of the train, would pull an empty car back through and into a position to be loaded by the tireless yarder. By the end of the day, all fourteen cars would be loaded by logs dragged in from the surrounding downed trees, if all went well. Seldom was there a perfect day.

The fallers and buckers worked well ahead of the rest, cutting down trees and removing their branches. They worked far from the crew to avoid crushing their fellow loggers under falling trees.

"Come on," said a sober Richard. "Let's find Big John."

Monty spotted him at the rear of the yarder preparing the boiler feeder so they could start logging the moment daylight would permit.

"Hey, John," Monty called out. "You know Don Brillo and Richard Swetzer. Tobias said to look you up when we got here."

"Well, you've found me and caught me in a good mood today. We finally have a full crew again. Monty, you and Richard will be setting chokers on the north side there. Don, can you handle the landing? Make sure the logs get stacked up right so the yarder can load 'em on the train."

"Sure."

"Do it then. Suppose you all know the whistles? One short whistle means stop, three shorts mean go ahead, and so on. Good. Joe Harbison is the whistle punk. He's a little stove up but he's forgotten more about logging than most men know."

That struck Monty as a back-handed sort of compliment which didn't inspire much confidence in Harbison's abilities, but he kept quiet and let John continue.

"Lunch will be brought out to the yarder from camp at noon. Don't be late."

A shrill blast from the yarder steam whistle sent all the men scattering. Monty and Richard headed out about one-quarter mile up the hill to where freshly-fallen logs were waiting for them. Joe stopped about half way up at a point of rock where he could see both the yarder and the two chokersetters. A small wire was laid from the yarder to the rock where Joe would spend the day. When he received a hand signal from one of the chokersetters, he would translate it into piercing whistles by a series of jerks on the wire, which would operate the steam whistle on the yarder. The series of short or long jerks would instruct the yarder man when and how to drag the log into the landing. The cable was as much as two inches in diameter and the power of the steam yarder was so prodigious that even a thirty-thousand-pound log would come flying in, pulling out whatever stumps that got entangled along the way. The whistle code included fast and slow, stop and start, and the most dreaded of all: a series of five long whistles for an accident. Lunch whistle was four short blasts and the most eagerly-awaited was six short ones: quitting time. In the summers the days were ten hours long, and the men usually worked six days a week.

Monty raised his hat as the signal to Joe that they were ready for the haul-back to send up another choker line. Joe transmitted this by two quick jerks on the whistle line. Almost immediately Chet Moyer released the haul-back drive brake and the two chokers were flying up the hill. Chet had worked in the woods all his life, and running a yarder was almost play to him. He handled the levers and clutches in much the manner that a good musician would play a violin.

Monty and Richard each unhooked a choker, snaked them under a log, slipped the nubbin in the bell to fasten them, hooked them to the main line, and stepped back as they signalled to Joe to haul away. Three short whistles rang out and in less than two minutes after sending the chokers up, Chet was dragging two large Doug fir logs down to the yarder at speeds of up to thirty miles an hour.

"Feels nice to be up here working again," remarked Monty as he swatted at some gnats. "I'd better get some repellant on 'cause in about an hour mosquitos big enough to carry you away will be zeroing in."

"Yeah, one thing about working up here, it sure will make me appreciate a beer tonight."

"As if he needed a reason," Monty thought sourly about his brother-in-law.

In a few minutes, four more chokers came up to them. After fastening them on one huge log and a few smaller ones, Joe blew the whistle again and the trees were on their way to the landing below.

"You know, Monty, every time I see Big John I know why he's called that."

Big John was indeed aptly named. At almost six feet tall and more than an axe handle broad, he lived with his mother who knew how to feed him. His usual breakfast was a dozen fried eggs and all the bacon he could eat, along with eight or ten hot cakes.

"Did you hear about Big John in that ruckus at Milford a couple weeks ago?" This from Richard.

"No, don't recollect it."

"Well, he was in the tavern having a beer and minding his own business. It was Saturday night and someone came in and told Big John a guy out in the parking lot wanted to whip him. Big John finished his beer, walked outside and over to this new '34 Ford Roadster. He said to the guy behind the wheel, 'Heard you might be interested in a little fight.'"

"'Maybe so. What's it to you?'"

"Big John opened the car door, jerked it off its hinges and threw it down in the gravel. The guy spun his wheels and left with gravel flying."

"Yeah, sounds like Big John Wooten, alright."
So the long day wore on.

7

As Monty and Richard walked over to join Joe Harbison for lunch break, Joe was thinking how glorious a June day this was in the Oregon woods. Despite his aches and pains, he knew if he had his life to live again it would be the same way. As he watched the two young men walk down the hill toward him, he was reminded of his youth.

"Monty, got anything special in that lunch bucket today?"

"Maybe so, Joe -- think Alice threw in an extra piece of huckleberry pie."

They sprawled out on a large boulder and soaked up a little early summer sun.

"You know," remarked Richard in a tired voice, "those chokers seem heavier every year. Guess I'm gettin' older."

"Hell, you don't know nothin' about getting older. Here I am almost seventy and back to being whistle punk -- the same thing I started out doing in the woods when I was fourteen years old. These lines and chokers are nothing compared to what I saw as a kid. Them days steel cable hadn't hardly been invented yet. Just hard-started using drums on the yarder. We were still using oxen or horses and pulling logs on a skid road. The yarder had a four-inch diameter rope on it to drag in logs. They hadn't thought of a haul-back yet, so we had to use a horse to pull rope back for another turn of logs. Them was the days, men were men and women were glad of it."

"Maybe we can trade places this afternoon," Richard jokingly suggested. "Darn, there goes that whistle again."

Back in Camp 18 the back-to-work whistle was barely heard. Gil Callahan had just driven into camp in his battered Dodge car looking for Tobe Tobias to have a show-down on his rail-laying contract. He stuck his head in the now-deserted mess hall, and hollered at no one in particular. "Hey, anybody here?"

A head poked out from the kitchen. "Just me, just me," replied the cook.

"Well, where's Tobe? They said he'd be up here."

"He's here alright. You just ain't looking in the right place. He's over there at that thing Gabe Hanks built and calls a bar." He pointed outside toward a small building slapped together from planks.

"Okay, okay -- any chance of getting a sandwich or something to eat?" Gil knew anybody who showed up at camp was welcome to food.

"Keep your shirt on. If you can stand warmed-up beef, here's some already made. Coffee's in the pot, milk is in the cooler. A few fresh strawberries in the dish there, from a patch in Haven. Early for berries yet, but they're fit to eat."

"Thanks, Andy. You're my kind of man."

Gil ate his lunch, then walked the hundred feet to the tavern. Inside it was quite dim, but appreciably cooler. The room was empty except for Tobe Tobias and Gabe Hanks, who were sitting at a bench table talking quietly.

"Well, well. If it ain't Mr. Money Pockets. How are you, Gil?"

"Couldn't be better, Tobe. Gabe, could you fix me up with a little whiskey and a glass of water?"

Dutifully Gabe provided the drinks. Gil drank greedily at first, but coughed and gasped before he finished.

Grinning, Gabe inquired, "What do you think of that batch, huh, Callahan?"

"Well, Gabe, I figure that drink was just about perfect."

Surprised, the barkeeper asked, "Perfect? How do you mean perfect?"

"It's this way, Gabe," Gil explained. "If that whiskey had been any better, you wouldn't have given it to me." He paused to swallow some water. "And if it'd been any worse, why, it would have killed me. So it was just right." Gabe Hanks cackled appreciatively, but Tobe studied Gil closely. Gil Callahan was barely middle-aged, but he had a world of work and experience behind him. He had gambled all his money (and that of many of his investors), and several years of his life building the railroad up the valley from Salem as far as this area. His black hair was beginning to show some gray, and his temper was moderating. His energy was waning, due mainly to his unending fear of losing the railroad and thus having nothing to show for his years of work and scheming.

Gabe placed another drink in front of Gil and remarked, "Did that five gallons of moonshine I sent over last week help mellow those fellows from back East?"

"It did, Gabe," replied Gil. "And I owe you one for it. That was pretty short notice I sent you."

Gil studied Gabe's retreating figure as he walked back behind the short bar. Gabe was of English stock, via Kentucky, and had turned out to be the black sheep of his family. He was a bachelor and a longtime purveyor of untaxed whiskey, which was welcome in most any home in the valley. He had curly hair, a well-dressed figure and an entertaining conversational manner. Gabe's flair for story-telling made him a hit with all the youngsters, both boys and girls.

In this room, at the end of the rail line, were gathered the three most successful -- and least trusted -- people around.

Tobe was watching Gil watching Gabe, and remarked in a soft voice, "You've probably figured out that if you need a little help persuading someone, Gabe's the man to call on?"

"Yeah. I guess he's helped both of us out of trouble. It's funny how a little whiskey can sometimes accomplish more than alot of hard work."

"What's on your mind, Gil? I know you didn't come up here to blab about whiskey."

"Can't say as I did. It's the contract on these spur logging lines I'm putting in for you. I can't make it on the price per mile you're paying me. Now, wait a minute, Tobe." Gil saw Tobe was about to interrupt. "Steel rail prices went up two dollars a ton last January, and the price you're charging me for sawing ties has almost doubled. I'm between a rock and a hard spot. You'll have to either pay me four hundred dollars more a mile for track laid or else furnish the ties free of charge. Take your pick."

"And what if I don't want to do either one? What would you do, Gil? Shoot yourself?"

"Listen to me, Tobe. You've got the largest sawmill in Oregon, have over four hundred men working for you, and lie and cheat to get timber for almost nothing. You can at least afford to pay a decent price for them spur lines."

"Quit your sniveling, Callahan. This isn't for general talking, but I'm so close to going under that I don't even know if I can make it through the summer.

Right now I'm scratching to come up with next month's payroll. Abner Brillo said the bank will not, and he emphasized the not, loan me any more money. I already owe him over a hundred thousand dollars, and I've got a snowball's chance in hell of getting any more out of him."

"That's hard to swallow, Tobe." Gil wearily wiped the sweat from his forehead. "Even if you get some other sucker to lay your rails, you'd have to pay a hell of a lot more than my price. I'd bet my bottom dollar you could do better by me than what you are."

Tobe studied Gil's sweating hands for a few moments and came to the conclusion that the railroad man was close to the breaking point. In fact, he was fed up with Gil's constant complaints and his attempts to up the agreed-on price; but he realized there was no guarantee that a newcomer wouldn't do the same thing, and finally decided that the devil he knew was better than the devil he didn't know.

"The very best I can do for you right now, Gil, is twenty bucks a mile more -- take it or leave it."

Gil reached for his empty glass, and slowly toyed with it. "Guess I'll have to take it, Tobe. I don't have to like it, but I have to take it."

Tobe turned his head toward the bar and saw that Gabe Hanks was listening to their conversation.

"Gabe, I know there's nothing wrong with your hearing, and if you ever repeat one word of what you heard here today -- I'll kill you. Now bring us a couple of drinks."

During the ensuing silence while the two men waited for their drinks, the faint sound of five long whistle blasts was heard in the bar; and again faintly, five more whistles: an accident. Tobias glanced across the table at Gil and left the bar without another word.

8

When Monty and Richard Swetzer returned to their chokersetting after lunch, the day was beginning to warm up. The clear-cut area was surrounded by standing timber, preventing any breeze from helping the loggers combat the heat of the tireless sun.

"I don't feel so good, Monty," moaned Richard as he ran behind a large log. "Must've ate too much lunch."

"In a pig's eye," Monty thought skeptically, as he heard retching sounds. He struggled to force the heavy choker under another log. "Won't he ever learn?" thought Monty. "You can't spend half the night in a tavern and still work hard the next day."

He gave the go-ahead signal and stepped back as another turn of logs headed for the yarder. Then he walked behind the log to check on Richard, who was passed out on the ground across a small rhododendron bush. Monty noted the regular breathing, decided to let him sleep it off, and returned to his work. The only problem was he would now have to perform for two men.

Monty began to sweat freely, and grabbed the water jug at every opportunity, as he strove to stay ahead of the powerful yarder's demand for logs. On the fourteenth turn of logs since lunch, it finally happened. He hooked the choker on a massive log -- the concentric circles of the wood's grain testified to its age -- gave the signal to go ahead, and started stepping back. By this time his freckles seemed to be popping out and his slight frame was trembling with fatigue. The log being pulled out struck the end of a smaller log and knocked it into an arcing swing. The swiftly-moving end caught Monty from behind on his right hip as he tried frantically to run farther back through the entangling brush. Suddenly all was deadly quiet in the area of felled trees.

After receiving no signals from the chokersetters for almost fifteen minutes, the whistle-punk finally walked uphill to the downed logs. Joe was pretty well out of breath when he arrived. He first discovered Richard down behind a log, apparently unconscious. After a quick search he discovered Monty barely moaning, lying face down beside a log.

Joe tried to roll Monty over, and the movement seemed to revive the injured man.

"My God, what happened, Monty?"

"I don't know, Joe. All I can remember is that log hit me from the back. Oh, that hurts. It feels like my leg must be broken clean off."

"No, it's still there. I'll get some help for both of you. Hang tough for awhile till I get back to my whistle wire."

Joe left at what was, for him, a run. After what seemed an interminable length of time, Monty heard five long blasts from the whistle and lapsed back into unconsciousness. Before he passed out again, he wondered what Joe meant about getting help for the both of them.

Within twenty minutes Big John and the yarder man arrived, carrying a brown canvas stretcher. Following them was Don Brillo with another stretcher. Joe Harbison was motioning toward where Monty lay on the ground. Big John carefully lifted him onto the stretcher. The pain brought a grimace to Monty's face, but he was not fully conscious.

"Don, you and Joe get Richard on a stretcher and we'll head out. They should have a speeder from Camp 18 at the yarder by the time we get there."

Monty attempted to sit up on his stretcher, but the excruciating pain forced him back with a gasp.

"How come Richard needs a stretcher? What's the matter with him?"

* * *

"Is Doc Golden in?" Big John was panting from his burden, speed and anxiety. We've got Monty Lewis here -- hurt pretty bad."

Doctor Golden appeared at the office door and finished drying his hands on a bloodied towel. "Bring him right on back. You'll have to excuse the mess, but I just had a man here with three fingers cut off at the sawmill."

The doctor led the way through a small corridor to the operating room or, as he preferred to call it, the patch-up room. The small three-bed hospital was neat and, for a sawmill-owned facility, fairly efficient. Arnold Golden had signed on as the company doctor in 1921 when he was fresh out of the east with a new license in medicine. The people in Milford and Haven had learned to rely on him and had grown to respect his abilities, both as a family doctor and as a friend.

Monty was quickly transferred from the stretcher to the hard table by Big John and Doctor Golden.

"What happened, John?"

"Don't know for sure, Doc. Richard Swetzer was settin' chokers with him but about all we could get from him was that Monty was hit by a log."

"You can help me, John, if you got the stomach for it."

"I can take it, Doc."

"First we've got to stop all this bleeding, and next --" Golden seemed to be talking more to himself now. "Going to be tough to save this leg, but I've got to do it, somehow. Monty and Alice seem more like kids of my own than anything else."

After what seemed an age, Monty was splinted and moved to a room nearby.

"I think we'll save the leg, John, but I'll have to wait for the swelling to go down before I can place a cast. I can assure you he'll be in here for quite a few days. Thanks for your help, John."

"That's okay, but if you're finished with me I'm going to have a long drink at Ned's Tavern -- I need it."

Big John entered the bar a few doors down from the hospital. "Evenin', Ned. How 'bout a little bourbon? Maybe a beer to wash it down."

"Comin' up. How's Monty getting along? Gabe was telling me you and Doc Golden were working on him."

Gabe Hanks, who had accompanied the stretcher from the camp as far as town, entered from a rear room and sat on the stool beside Big John. In a moment Tobe Tobias joined them.

John responded to Ned. "Doc thinks he'll come out of it, maybe a bad limp, though."

Gabe shook his head. "Richard Swetzer says it was mostly Monty's fault. He got careless and didn't step back far enough when that log was jerked out. Richard was busy hooking on another log and didn't see everything that happened."

"Bullshit. When we got there, Richard was passed out behind a log and you could smell the whiskey ten feet away. He didn't even know Monty had been hurt. It took about a bucket of water to bring him around." Big John aimed for a spittoon by his feet.

"You mean Richard was letting Monty do all the work when this happened?" This from now wide-awake Tobias.

"You got it."

"Well that's the end of Swetzer working for me." Tobias got up to leave with this parting remark: "And if I have my way I'll see to it he never works another day in the valley."

9

With a honk and a cloud of dust the Model T rolled to a stop in front of Alice's house in Haven.

"Be right out, Don." Alice appeared at the front door briefly. In a moment she was shooing Josh and Mary towards the car. "Sure thank you for taking us into Milford -- we get to bring Monty home today. Isn't that wonderful?"

"Sure thing, Alice." Don Brillo, Abner's brother, was forced to smile, for Alice's happiness was contagious. "She sure is a fighter for her family," he thought, "and tough as nails to boot. The world needs more like her."

The trip to Milford from Haven was pleasant on this summer morning. The wild blackberries permeated the air with their ripe perfume, which reminded Alice that canning time should be in full swing. Huckleberries would soon be ripe and, with luck, Monty would be able to go with them for the picking high up in the mountain meadows.

Monty was waiting, impatiently, on the large front porch when they arrived. He shrugged off their help while he struggled up from the chair to his crutches. As he hobbled down the steps to the car, Doctor Golden opened the front door of the hospital and motioned for Alice to come in. Rather apprehensively, Alice entered his office.

"Come on, smile again, Alice. Monty will be okay."

Alice forced a smile. "You know me, Dr. Golden, just a worry wart. But Monty looks so helpless now with those big crutches."

"Stop worrying. He can probably shed those in a couple of weeks. But I do have some advice for you. Monty should never work in the woods again."

"Oh, don't say that." Alice was almost in tears. "I'd love to get him away from that work, but it will almost kill him to quit logging."

"That's just it, Alice. With that injured leg, he'll either hurt the leg some more or he'll be in an accident because of it failing him some time. He'll probably limp for at least a year, but he might forever if he goes back to the woods and hurts it again."

"Have you told him?"

"No, I thought it'd be better if you broke the news to him, Alice. But I do know there will be an opening at the bank in a few weeks, and Monty would be just the man for that cashier job. I happen to know that Gil Callahan thinks alot of Monty, and has already put in a good word for him to Abner Brillo."

"Say, that's great news! That way, he won't feel so helpless waiting for this to heal."

Alice gave the doctor a quick hug, went outside and eased into the back seat beside Monty. "Let's go, Don. I want to get this big lunk home."

* * *

Autumn breathed a new sort of life into the mountains. Blackbirds gathered together in the tens of thousands for migration south. They would burden tree limbs to the point of breaking, then block out vast expanses of sky and fill the air with a cacophonous rushing and squawking as they took off. Geese, too, were on the move, their lopsided vee formations black against the fall clouds, their cries of instruction and encouragement to each other clearly audible on the ground. The few deciduous trees colored and lost their leaves, but the giant fir trees remained as implacably dark as ever.

On one of these early fall days a man stopped his touring car at the only pay phone in Linnton. After pulling out a handful of change he rang the operator and asked to place a call to a number in San Francisco.

"That will be thirty five cents for the first minute, please."

A tinkle of change was heard, and then, "Hello, is this Tony Ansca? Never mind who I am, just listen. I've got a job for you -- an easy thousand dollars. I heard about you from Gabe Hanks. Good. If you want this job, it'll just take a few days. Now listen."

"That will be another sixty cents for three more minutes, please."

"Yes, yes, here it is."

"You still there, Tony? Take a train up to Milford. On September twenty-fourth go to Gabe Hanks' new cabin at the foot of Coffin Mountain. Ask someone here where it is, anybody can tell you. Sound okay to you? Good. Don't forget -- the twenty-fourth."

The man backed out of the pay station, looked rather furtively around and rapidly drove away.

By the middle of September, Monty had commenced his new position as cashier in the bank. He was apprehensive when he entered the bank, for his adult work-life had centered on timber-related work, not pens and ink and corn counters. Evidently old Abner Brillo could sense this in the young man who was limping into the cool interior of the building.

"Glad to see you, Monty. Come on back here and meet Pete Justin. He'll be staying on another week to get you used to the feel of money, so to speak."

"Thanks, Mr. Brillo. You'll never regret hiring me, although pushing a pencil will be some different than rolling a log."

"Don't worry, Monty." Abner patted his shoulder. "Anyone who can have children as nice as yours can do anything. Justin, would you show Monty how to be a top notch cashier like you?"

Monty marveled at the amount of money in the cage -- bills up to one hundred dollars each, which he had never laid eyes on before. To his right was a wooden rack of silver dollars and in the bottom drawer under the currency were the gold eagles and double eagles. In the west not all people had learned to accept paper money; some reluctantly, some not at all.

"Hello, Monty. Could I have some change for this twenty?" Gil Callahan had appeared at Monty's window, and peeled one from a small roll of bills. "You were on the way to the hospital pretty well bunged up the last time I saw you."

"Five, ten, twenty. Yes, I feel real good now. Doc says I'll be rid of this limp in a few months."

Justin had walked into the vault for a moment and the counter was empty of customers when Gil leaned over and remarked in a low voice, "You boys did a good piece of work with that dynamite." He left before Monty could reply.

The day passed rather quickly for Monty. Most of the customers knew him and many shook his hand and wished him well. Late in the afternoon, Richard Swetzer dropped in and spoke to Monty.

"How would you like to buy a good Model T Ford, Monty? Old man Crossburn has one for sale and it's a good one -- only wants forty dollars for it."

"What color is it, Richard?"

"You know what Henry Ford always says -- you can buy a Ford in any color you want, as long as it's black."

"Yeah," Monty laughed, "I'll be done in an hour or so. Stick around and we'll take a look at it. I'll have to get something to drive from Haven every day."

Monty and Richard walked down to Crossburn's mansion on a small hill overlooking the Chinook River. Monty's ring at the door was answered by a man whom Monty hardly recognized. The Crossburn at the door looked only a little like the man Monty had seen in the mill in the spring. Art asked Monty into the parlor.

"You're looking very well, Monty." He attempted a smile as he motioned toward a sofa. The smile showed dark gums around his elongated teeth. Monty thought to himself that Art looked much older than his fifty-some years. His thinning hair, trembling hands, and gray color combined to accentuate his premature aging.

"My God," thought Monty, "he's an old man already."

"I've always admired your home, Mr. Crossburn," Monty observed as he put off the subject of his visit. "Those turrets at the corners of the roof and the wide porch around three sides with all the gingerbread are just beautiful. This is the first time I've seen the inside of it."

"Kind of you to say so, Monty. My wife and I have always enjoyed it. It's a big house and lots of work. At my age sometimes too much."

"I came about that Model T you have for sale."

"Right there in the garage. It's in good shape, but I'm getting too old to drive anymore. Hope you buy it. You seem the type of person who would take good care of it. It's yours for forty dollars."

After a few more polite phrases, they went out to inspect the car. Monty raised the hood, tried the clutch and brake, sat in the seat and surprised himself by saying, "I'll take it, Mr. Crossburn. If you say it's okay that's good enough for me. Stop by the bank in the morning and I'll have the money for you -- one of the benefits of having a steady job! Boy, will Alice be surprised!"

The next day Monty proudly drove his newly-purchased car to Milford for the first time. There was an empty spot beside the bank, seemingly made for parking his car. Alice had been as surprised and pleased as he'd hoped. After all, she admitted later to him, she had always appreciated the speeder rides with her father into town, but it didn't seem too ladylike anymore. "Not that I'm getting hoity-toity," she'd added.

Monty removed his cash boxes and coin holders from the vault and was ready for the day's business when the front door to the bank was unlocked. Albert Toonan came to Monty's window to make his weekly deposit. Two other people were waiting in line behind him when Gil Callahan noisily wheeled a hand cart through the front door.

"Where's Abner Brillo?" he demanded. "I've got some money to deposit."

"What can I do for you, Gil?" asked Abner as he emerged from his back office.

"Here's sixty-two thousand dollars you can put in your vault for me. Just leave this box locked and I'll pick it up in a couple weeks. That's money from new stock holders in my railroad. It's on to Bend now with the rails!"

He smiled good-naturedly to the bank customers as he helped Abner carry the strongbox to the vault.

51

After the box was safely stored in the vault, Gil walked through the bank to the front door waving hellos and joking with the waiting customers.

When Monty re-entered his cashier's cage after a brief lunch, a man was waiting to see him. "Excuse me, but could you tell me how to find Gabe Hanks' cabin? It's somewhere near Coffin Mountain, I guess."

"It's about an hour's walk from here. Follow this street," Monty motioned to the front of the bank, "until you come to Rock Creek -- follow that trail up the creek for about two miles. You'll know when you get there. The trail ends. You'll be right under Coffin Mountain and the creek turns into a high water fall. The cabin is not far from the foot of the fall. Made from hand-split boards with a cedar shake roof. You won't find Gabe there today, though. He told me this morning he was heading to Salem to make a delivery to, um, a customer."

The stranger thanked Monty, and as he left the bank Monty stared thoughtfully at his retreating back.

The man had no trouble finding the trail on Rock Creek, but as it was a warm day he soon removed his sweater. His clothing was not of an outdoor type and his shoes were made more for sidewalks than anything else. The trail soon entered the old growth trees, and the sun was effectively blotted out. When the stranger to the valley arrived at Gabe's cabin, he silently circled it to verify that Gabe indeed was away, remembering the instructions on the phone not to talk to Gabe.

"Anybody here?" he shouted. Hearing no answer, he tried the front door and was surprised to find it unlocked. He entered the large one-room cabin to await his visitor. A sheet of paper spread on the table drew his attention.

"Hi Tony." The scrawling was difficult to read. "I couldn't wait any longer but here is what I want you to do." Ansca studied the note carefully. It had no signature. He stuffed the note in his pocket and left on the return journey to Milford.

After the children were tucked in bed that night, Monty retrieved his dad's old journal from the buffet drawer and continued his writing.

> Today was an interesting day at the bank. Gil Callahan came in early this morning and deposited $62,000 in our vault. Said it was from investors in his railroad so he could continue it finally to Bend, and that he'd be leaving for a few days to San Francisco to round up some material and men for the work. Also a couple hours later a man in the bank asked me directions to Gabe Hank's place by Coffin Mountain. He was a stranger, nothing to write home about, but he sure gave me the heebie-jeebies. Also Art Crossburn came in this afternoon and I paid him the rest of the forty dollars for the car he'd sold me. His hands were shaking so bad he could hardly sign a receipt for it. Don't look like he's long for this world. Finally got that gold tooth in that I wanted for a while -- pretty sharp, if I do say so myself. Things sure are looking up -- almost too good to be true.

10

As the moon topped the ridge east of Haven, Tony Ansca was knocking at the door of a small house.

"I was told to see you and that you'd have all the explanations for this job."

A coal oil lamp was lighted, and Tony surveyed the sparse furniture in the room. Not much and mostly hand-me-down stuff, he figured.

"What's all this about, anyway?" asked Tony. "I'm completely in the dark. All I know this guy called and promised me a bunch of money to help him on something here."

The man holding the oil lamp scrutinized Tony. "I thought you'd know who he was. All I know about him is a couple letters he sent. But none of them were signed or had a return address. Did have a Salem postmark."

"Hell's bells," remarked Tony. "What did he promise you?"

"It was a little indefinite but it mentioned splitting a big bundle of money when the job was done. That's all I need to hear."

Tony thought a moment before replying. "He promised me a thousand for my part. For that kind of money I'm willing to take a chance. What are we supposed to do?"

"He wants us to throw together a little pole shack up in the woods. I know the place -- a trail brings you right to it. It's out of the way, alright. You can get to it without being seen by anybody."

"When does he want it done?" Tony was planning to complete his part, whatever it might be.

"Wants the shack finished by day after tomorrow. He'll have a letter waiting at Milford on that day telling us what to do next."

"Suits me. I'd like to know who's behind it but what the hell? I ain't picky. Suppose you have an axe, hammer, and a few nails around." Tony was ready. "I might as well stay here tonight and we can start early in the morning. Got any grub around?"

"Yup, a little. This guy included a hundred dollars in the letter. I used some of that. Come to think of it, he must have been pretty sure I'd go along with this."

By the end of the second day the two men had developed a few blisters along with some tired muscles, for manual labor was not their strong suit. As they drove into Milford on the way home, they stopped by the post office and picked up the mail.

"Another letter postmarked in Salem," Ansca observed. "He must have known we'd bust our butts to get that shack done by tonight."

When they had returned to the house and had dipped into a quart of home-brewed beer, Tony tore open the letter.

* * *

Milford was its usual quiet self at 1:45 Friday afternoon. A black touring car was parked across from the bank. No one was on the street except for a man leaning against a porch post at the drug store. There were a few customers in the stores and several in the bank. A man emerged from the touring car. He looked out of place on this sunny fall day in his black rain coat and felt hat pulled down over his eyes. He quickly pulled a bandana up to his eyes and motioned to the man in front of the drugstore, who limped over to join him. This man also pulled a kerchief over his face. He wore a black hat that obscured the upper part of his face, and denim pants. After a moment or two of discussion, they walked across the street and entered the bank.

Some twenty minutes later Abner Brillo was recounting the events of the afternoon for the sheriff, who recorded it word for word in a lined composition book like the children used in the local school.

"They almost knocked the door down when the two of them came in. The little guy said it was a hold-up and for nobody to move. Their revolvers looked as big as buffalo guns. The bigger one headed for me -- had a limp, ya know -- and told me to take him to the vault while the other guy covered us from the front door. The vault door was unlocked and I swung it open. 'Stick all that paper money in a bank sack and don't tell me you don't have one.' That's what he said, word for word. So I did. Then he made me help him carry that strongbox to the front door, him toting the money sack, too."

Brillo continued the tale. "The other one said, 'Let's get outta here,' but the first one ran back to the cage to see what was there. He demanded all the money there from Barney Pritchart, including any in the drawers. Poor old Barney was cool as a cucumber; pretended to be doing what he said, but instead he slipped a brass paper weight from the lower drawer and all of a sudden hit the crook in the face with it. It made a bad cut and drew some blood, because I could see it running down by his ear. I thought for a minute the guy was going to shoot Pritchart then and there, but instead he just glared at him and with that limping run made a dash for the front door. Took some guts for Barney to do that," Abner added mournfully.

He mopped his forehead with a handkerchief and continued. "When they reached the front door, the guy with the limp whirled around and fired one shot into the bank and I'll be darned if it didn't hit Pritchart. Killed him almost instantly." Abner took a long drink of water. "Sure wish I had something stronger than this, Sheriff."

Hearing no offer in response to his hint, Brillo picked up the story again. "The two must have piled into a car cause we could hear the gravel flying as they left."

"Anybody know which direction they took?" asked the sheriff of the crowd trying to get in the bank.

"Went right by my store," shouted Toonan, "heading east. If you hurry you might still get 'em."

* * *

Alice was ladling oatmeal into bowls for Mary and Josh's breakfast when she first noticed the sheriff's car drive up.

"What on God's green earth is he doing here so early in the morning?" she said to the children, feeling vaguely anxious.

"Good morning, Mrs. Lewis. May I ask you a few questions?"

"Why, yes. Anything."

"I'd rather they'd be in private, Mrs. Lewis. maybe we could step out in the yard for a minute." They did so, with Alice admonishing the children to eat all their breakfast.

"Now, we need to know where your husband was yesterday, Alice."

"Why, he went to Portland on some bank business. Late Thursday Barney Pritchart called from the bank and said he and Monty were leaving right away for a bank examiner's hearing. I think that's what he called it. Anyhow, he said they would be in Portland all day Friday and probably wouldn't be home until sometime Saturday. I'm expecting him back soon."

"I'm afraid there's a misunderstanding here, Mrs. Lewis." The sheriff had returned to the more formal mode of address. "You see, Barney Pritchart was killed in a Milford bank robbery yesterday, and about eight or ten people have identified Monty as being one of the robbers and the killer of Pritchart."

Alice's face blanched and as her knees sagged she clutched at the sheriff for support. "You're crazy, Sheriff. Monty couldn't and wouldn't do a thing like that. When he gets home this will all be straightened out. You'll see."

"Well, when you see him be sure and tell him we need to talk to him. We searched all evening yesterday and finally found the car they drove abandoned on an old logging road east of here. It was stolen from Salem. Looks like they left it behind and took off on horseback. No one has seen them since."

The sheriff drove away as Alice slowly walked back into her house. "Mary, I want you and Josh to run up to Papa's and ask him to come down right away. Tell him I need his help. Now! Hurry."

Soon after Gus Swetzer arrived at Alice's with the two children, the phone rang: a short, a long and a short, the Lewis' ring. The sheriff was on the line and informed Alice they had just picked up Monty walking east of Haven and he was on his way to jail in Salem, where he would be charged with bank robbery and murder.

Alice was too stunned to answer. She slowly hung up the phone. "Papa!" was all she said.

11

1964

The Chinook River, hardly more than a creek so near its mountain headwaters, leapt and cavorted near the road with unusual energy, thanks to the beginnings of the snow melt. Warren Ascott's pickup rattled comfortably along. It was well into the shabby stage and rapidly approaching the decrepit, but he still felt good in it, high off the road and independent enough to tackle the rougher logging roads as well as the bumpy county roads, and the few paved state highways around. He had travelled over one hundred thousand miles in this rig, and could account for almost every hole and rip in the upholstery of the wide bench seat (there he had sat with a screwdriver in his back pocket, here a hunting knife had protruded from a rucksack), every pit in the windshield (a logging truck had thrown a rock up at him on Doublerock Road four -- no, five years ago, and that one up in the corner came from the Olafson boy's beebee gun, just last month).

Monty's journal rested on the seat beside Warren, bouncing occasionally at a chuck hole. Warren had intended to skim through it at the Milford Library, but curiosity got the better of him. He slowed and pulled onto a wide, gravelly plateau just above the river, turned off the engine, rolled down a window, and picked up the journal. With the quiet yet lively rumble of the Chinook in his ears, he thumbed through the few pages of 1964.

Alice was right; Monty was obsessed with "solving" the Milford bank robbery. He wrote of nothing else: not of his first freedom in thirty years, not of his wife or the spring air or his children and grandchildren. Unfortunately, there was no indication in the sparse entries of Monty's intentions, nor any explanation of his disappearance. Only that cryptic reference to a face from thirty years back was puzzling. Had Monty's singleness of purpose led him to imagine things? Warren remembered Monty as the picture of stability, but then that was before three decades of seeing life behind brick walls with barbed wire and broken glass on the top. *Now it's my turn.* What did Monty mean by that?

Warren sighed and flipped pages, trying not to notice the gap between 1934 and 1964. He quickly reached the right year, and settled on the entry dated January 4, 1934. Soon he was oblivious to the river's voice, the too-cool breeze blowing in the open window, and the gentle knocks and pings the pickup engine made as it cooled down. He was seeing the Depression through Monty's eyes, and hearing, as if reverberated down a narrow canyon, the echoes of the young Monty's life.

Warren read a few entries and then lay the journal aside. He felt uncomfortable at this probing into Monty's life, but even more uncomfortable at recognizing the probable motive in Monty's crimes: he needed money. It was as simple as that. The robbery, Warren recalled, took place in the early fall. Monty had sold his traps to see them through the winter, and come spring and summer he could have hunted and fished to keep his family fed, even gorged. But fall would have brought the renewed threat of winter. What would Monty do then? What else could he sell? Pawning jewelry was impossible, for the simple reason that the Lewises had none. Hocking the rifle was out of the question, as that brought in a good part of their food in the form of wild game. Even getting rid of the traps in order to buy necessities for the winter had been a sacrifice sale, a desperate move that would deprive Monty of sorely-needed supplemental income from the beaver skins he must have sold or traded. There would be no seasonal work for Monty in the winter, no logging in the woods that surrounded Milford, no haying or harvesting on the few farms around, no carpentry, no selling vegetables from their garden, no road work -- no work at all. Warren felt that the journal could argue only against Monty's innocence, but he picked it up again and continued.

Apparently Monty had no set schedule for making entries. From time to time he would jot down his thoughts, which seemed to focus on the economic hardship of the times. Warren read for awhile, then once again put the journal down, and this time noticed the cold. He got out to stretch his legs, then got back in, rolled up the window, turned the pickup and heater on, and found the next entry. To his surprise, things seemed to have picked up for the Lewises. Monty had let several months go by without writing in his journal; but the change for the better, when it came at last, was fully and happily recorded.

> September 10, 1934. I got a job! It'll be my first steady job since '32, and the best one I've ever had. Abner Brillo came up to me at the Independence Day picnic, just before the horse race was due to start, and said he needed another teller at the Milford Bank and that he'd heard good things about me, and would I like the job? I thought he was pulling my leg at first -- like he had to ask if I wanted a job! But he meant every word. I guess as manager he has a pretty free hand in who to hire. Said he was making Pritchart assistant manager, that he had all the makings of an "executive." I had sense enough not to say that being Brillo's second cousin twice removed, or whatever it

is, wasn't bad in the way of makings. But who cares? Thanks to that I got the job, started yesterday in fact. Not much to it, really. A good bit easier than falling trees or digging ditch, and the old Milford one-room school taught me plenty of arithmetic to tote up what comes in in these parts. Wonder who'd been talking to old Brillo about me? I'd sure give him a slap on the back if I knew. A steady job -- just like in the old days. Seems almost too good to be true.

Warren skimmed quickly over the next few entries. It seemed as though good fortune motivated Monty to write in more detail. Throughout August and September he had recorded fairly thoroughly his contentment in his meager victories in life: the daily pleasures of counting money (Monty never mentioned plain old cash, only "hard cash"), the building of an entirely new springhouse, the repurchase of his beaver traps, Josh's catching on the baseball team, Mary's rendering of "Red River Valley" on the concertina, Alice's second prize in the Linnton quilt show. Monty recorded even the trivial adversities: Mary's summer cold, the blight on the rose bushes, his own trip to the dentist to get a gold tooth: a molar. The easy summer living with its plenty of game, fruit, vegetables and flowers combined with Monty's long-awaited return to financial stability, or at least a few dollars tucked away for a rainy day, to render that late summer of '34 -- in the middle of the Great Depression -- an idyllic time for the Lewis family. Monty hadn't said it precisely that way, but Warren read it between the lines.

Then the fall came.

12

It was with difficulty that Warren left behind the summer of '34 and returned to the tail end of the present winter. Monty's journal stopped abruptly in September, and contained not a single reference to the robbery. Warren reflected that that was hardly surprising; Monty must have had slightly more pressing matters on his mind than keeping his journal up to date. All the same, it was disappointing. Warren shifted into gear and continued his drive.

The town of Linnton loomed ahead of him suddenly. It was perched on the flank of Coffin Mountain, so named for the appearance of its flat top which, from a distance, looked like a casket respectfully elevated on an altar-stand. Indeed, from Warren's vantage point the top of the mountain looked perfect in its smoothness and evenness. Another coffin caught his eye: the wooden sign of Linnton's local mortuary- furniture store. Not exactly a tasteful sign, Warren decided, and an odd combination of businesses for Otto Moyer. Right next door was the office and home of Dr. Arnold Golden, Jr. Doc Golden and, before him, his father, had delivered most of the babies in the Linnton area, pulled most of the teeth, lanced most of the boils and sold most of the eyeglasses for the last forty-five years. Warren chuckled at Doc Golden's proximity to the Moyer establishment.

The trip out Linnton way was necessitated by the dearth of old newspapers at the Milford Public Library. Abigail Toonan, Milford's librarian, church organist and sole vegetarian, informed the ranger tartly that her library could not afford subscriptions to frivolous publications, which category apparently included the *Linnton Standard*. Warren bowed to Mrs. Toonan's superior knowledge of frivolity in periodicals; after all, she had once had a letter to the editor published in the *Capitol Times*, Salem's daily newspaper, on the undesirability of the modern hymns in Sunday Service. When Warren had pointed out that, in fact, a Linnton newspaper was quite unnecessary since everybody in town new everybody else's business long before it reached the ears of the *Standard*'s newsman -- Warren paused before the word as if he doubted its accuracy in this case -- Mrs. Toonan unbent sufficiently to confide that that odd Mr. Hanks kept every single thing he could get his hands on, and probably still had every issue the *Standard* had ever printed. Under Warren's bantering influence, Mrs. Toonan conceded that the *Standard* might have its uses, if not for reporting what went on, then at least for chronicling who got caught at it. On that note, and after a small contribution to the church choir fund, Warren reseated himself in his trusty pickup and headed for Linnton and the ramshackle cabin of Gabe Hanks.

Gabe was remote in more ways than one. As Warren passed through Linnton and on up Coffin Mountain, he recalled the various phases of Gabe's career. Judging by his accent Gabe must have been born in the south. He claimed Kentucky as his birthplace, although apparently Kentucky didn't claim him. In fact, word had it that not only unrelated Kentuckians, who might be presumed to be unbiased in the matter, had run Gabe out of the state; Warren had heard that even the Hanks clan itself was ready to eject Gabe forcibly from the county, and only a fast horse had saved him from being tarred and feathered by his own brothers, sisters, cousins, second cousins, first cousins twice removed, and other assorted relations that are counted as kin in Kentucky. Warren didn't know how much of that tale to credit, but he did know from emphatic locals something of Gabe's history since his arrival in Linnton in 1925.

Supposedly Gabe had quickly established himself as the local moonshiner, supplying the better part (depending on your point view, Warren reflected) of the county with rotgut whisky of such debatable quality that Doc Golden (Old Man Golden, of course, not Junior) enjoyed a noticeable surge in business during Gabe's tenure. His social life was said to consist of endearing himself to lonely women whose husbands were away for long stretches at the logging camps. Gabe's success in this endeavor was predictably spotty, given his commitment to bathing once a month whether he needed it or not. Nonetheless, he must have prevailed at least once, to go by the bullets that riddled his still one rainy night which, together with the end of Prohibition in '33, reduced but didn't terminate his entrepreneurial activity.

Eventually his ardor and his ambition both decreased, and he made do on odd jobs and errands for others, widely interspersed between periods of idleness. He also scavenged, more thoroughly than anyone Warren had even known. Gabe roamed not only towns in search of odds and ends to pick up, but also the vast territory of woods and mountaintops around Linnton, Milford and Campton. He had amassed a huge variety of junk in this manner, and had a scout's knowledge of the area. People preferred his wilderness roving to his town visits, as he was not terribly particular about the details of ownership. In short, Mrs. Toonan's description of Gabe Hanks as a "shiftless hound" was not far wrong.

The way to the Hanks cabin led Warren along ever-narrower roads and lanes, until finally the brush on either side was scraping along the length of the pickup. Warren had almost concluded that he had made a wrong turn, when he emerged from the brush and into a clearing. Nestled, or rather leaning, against the woods at the back of the clearing was the cabin. Warren climbed down from the driver's seat and shouted toward the structure.

"Hey, Gabe! Hallo! Anybody to home?"

There was a slight shuffling sound from the trees behind the cabin, and presently a grey head appeared around a corner, followed shortly by a tall, spindly body.

"Who's inquirin'?" The fellow looked old, probably older than he really was, Warren decided.

"It's me, Gabe. Warren Ascott. Don't you remember? I gave you a lift into town once or twice. I'm the ranger out of Campton."

Gabe peered at Warren and meditated for a few moments. "You say out Campton way?"

"Right. Don't you recognize my truck?"

The scrutiny was shifted to the pickup, then back to Warren. "Yup. I got you now. You all's the one who chased me out of them meadows above Campton, just for building a bitty old fire to roast some fresh venison. What you want here?" Gabe shifted his weight to a more comfortable position, and suddenly Warren realized that Gabe was leaning on a hunting rifle, definitely antique but probably still functional.

"Uh, well now, Gabe, I had to do that. Right smack in fire season, you know. High forest fire danger. Very high. Uh, you know how that is." Warren had completely forgotten about that incident, and was unpleasantly surprised to find that Gabe hadn't. "After all, we get a big fire going and your place here would be one of the first to go up in smoke."

Gabe didn't look convinced, but he grunted and jabbed a thumb at a pile of wooden slats that Warren only then recognized as a chair.

"Lawn furniture! How nice." Warren strode forward and sat, rightly interpreting Gabe's gesture as an invitation. "Beautiful spot you've got here, Gabe. Suits you to a T."

"I like it," Gabe admitted grudgingly. "Tain't half bad. Not so good's it used to be, damned chimney's leaning. Well's got muddy. But it still ain't half bad."

Warren nodded, then jumped as his host quickly reached down under Warren's legs and deftly produced a green-tinted Mason jar partly full of a bilious-looking liquid. Gabe unscrewed the cap and shoved the jar at the ranger. Hazarding a guess as to what this odd man was displaying so proudly, Warren said heartily,

"Ah! Fertilizer. For your fine garden there, naturally." He waved toward a few scraggly strawberry bushes and some tired-looking beans. Gabe laughed wheezily and shook his head.

"No? Not fertilizer. Cleaning fluid, then. You'll be doing spring cleaning about now." Gabe wheezed again.

"Oh, I got it now," Warren said desperately. "It's an experiment. You're working on a, uh, a new kind of fuel. Right?"

Gabe bent over and slapped Warren's knee ferociously, causing Warren to start so that a small amount of the liquid splashed onto his hands.

"Hey! Don't be slopping it around like that." Gabe rescued the jar from his guest and, to Warren's surprise and disgust, swigged some of it down. "But you can have your fun on me if you like. Old Gabe don't mind, when he's got a body to share a drink with. Go ahead." Once again Warren found himself holding the jar.

"Gee, thanks alot, Gabe. But I couldn't. No, really, I couldn't. I just had a rotten prune." He smiled weakly at Gabe. "Actually, I'm here to discuss an important matter. I need to look at some old issues of the *Linnton Standard*, way back to the '30s, and I heard you might have some. I need to take a look at the stories on the Milford Bank Robbery in '34. Remember that?"

After looking glum for a few seconds, Gabe had regained his cheerfulness. "Hah. Course I remember. Read about that meself, sometimes. Saw a story about that there robbery just the other day."

"What? You mean you do have the newspapers? Can I see them? It would mean alot to me, Gabe." Warren smiled in what he hoped was a friendly and winning way.

"Got every durn story that fish-wrap of a paper ever wrote on it. Course," here Gabe paused and grinned cunningly, "Course, wouldn't show 'em to just anybody. But maybe I would to, oh, say ... a drinking buddy."

Warren had seen it coming, but made one last attempt to save himself. "There's reason in that, Gabe. There's reason in that. But you see, I can't be your drinking buddy because, well, because of my stomach!" The ranger was pleased with this inspiration. "That's it, you see. My stomach. Can't take alcohol in any way, shape or form. Nosirree. Not even the fine stuff that you produce."

Gabe shook his head sadly. "Too bad." He headed back toward the woods.

"No, hang on, there, Gabe." Rising from the chair, Warren held out his hand bravely. Gabe laughed his unsettling laugh again, wiped the lip of the jar on his sleeve, and handed the potion over. Warren took a deep breath and, before exhaling, took a long swallow of the stuff. Choking back a cough, he returned the jar and mustered up some enthusiasm. "My, my, that certainly is something, Gabe. Yes indeed. Definitely something!"

Satisfied, Gabe led the way into the dim and musty interior of the cabin. "Them papers is right in here. Help yourself."

Halting at the threshold to let his eyes adjust, Warren put his hand carelessly on a small plank table against the wall. Something swished slowly on the table, and Warren peered in the direction of the movement. "What's that on your table, here, Gabe? Seems to be moving." Warren stepped closer, then leaped back. "Mother of God! What is that thing? Looks like a young alligator!" He took another step back, and wiped his hand on his pants. "I think I touched it." Quickly Gabe scooped the creature up, and started crooning to it paternally. "There, Molly, don't pay him no mind. You're okay, you are."

Warren edged forward and, his eyes accustomed to the darkened room, gazed curiously at the animal. "Gabe, what on earth is that? It's too big to be a lizard and too small to be a dinosaur." Gently Gabe extended his hands to show his Molly to better advantage. "You mean you never seen an old Molly Crobottom, Ranger? Never even heard of 'em?"

No longer afraid, Warren stared at the strange pet. "Never seen one, never heard of one. Is it some kind of lizard?"

Gabe shrugged his shoulders. "Beats me. Don't think so, though. Lizards are quick, disappear in nothin' flat. Molly here is slow as they come. Watch her walk." Molly was deposited back on the table, and prodded unceremoniously from behind. She swung her reptilian head around, darted out her tongue, and then slowly -- so slowly Warren was amazed -- she moved her right front leg; and then her left front leg; and then her right back leg; and then the left back leg. She stopped, as if done in.

Both men stood in silent appreciation, Gabe as proud as if his Molly had won a race.

"Are there many around?" Warren inquired.

Again Gabe shrugged. "Here it's only Molly and me. I seen a few others, mostly down lower though. Don't know where they come from or where they go." Gabe glanced sidelong at Warren. "Ready to take a gander at them papers now?"

Reluctantly, Warren pulled his gaze away from Molly.

"You bet, Gabe. Lead on."

Gabe sat down on a chair that seemed to be the mate of the one out front. "Nowhere to lead, Ranger. Look around."

Puzzled, Warren did so. He saw no cabinet or desk that might conceal the papers, no closet or chest of drawers. The only piece of furniture besides Molly's table and Gabe's chair was a tiny but ornate pot-bellied wood stove, mounted on four curved legs that ended in tiny hooved feet. Gabe smiled and swung his arm about him. Finally it dawned on Warren: the entire room was literally papered over -- in newspapers. Every wall was covered in newsprint, every visible inch of space taken up with the *Linnton Standard*. Gabe pointed his finger and Warren looked up; even the ceiling was covered with them.

13

The clinking of dishes and the smell of coffee, onions and stew drifted from the kitchen of Kate's Restaurant out to where Warren faced his friend, Earl Millican, across a formica-topped table. It was the Saturday lunch rush in Campton, which meant that there were three diners in the place besides Earl and Warren. Kate bustled in and out of the dining area, filling water glasses and promoting her blue plate special. The little restaurant was comfortably warm, with that Saturday feeling that made a person want to stretch and yawn and have another cup of coffee. Warren turned his head to catch Kate's eye, winced and put a hand to the back of his neck.

"Say, Earl, get Kate over here with that coffee pot, would you?"

"What's a matter? Your arm broken?" Earl waved to attract Kate's attention, and mimed the pouring.

"No, but I think my neck darn near is. I spent three hours yesterday reading Gabe's walls. You know that cabin of his has four rooms, and one of them goes on for ever. Whenever he needs more space he just throws together another room, and goes on until he runs out of lumber. That wasn't the worst of it, though. What really got to me was reading the ceiling. I had to stand on a table that wobbled every time I breathed, with a notebook in one hand, a pen in the other and a flashlight under one arm so I could see to read. Plus I had to watch where I put my feet to avoid squishing Molly."

"Molly? Who the devil is Molly?"

"Just Gabe's pet. A Molly Crobottom," said Warren, preparing to explain.

"Oh, yeh."

"Come on now, Earl. Don't tell me you know what one is. I practically jumped out of my skin when I saw it."

Earl smiled. "Sure I know. Had one myself when I was a kid. Mom didn't think much of it, but it was better than a snake or a frog, so she took the lesser evil and let me keep it. But why were you hobnobbing with Gabe, anyway? Forest Service business?"

"Naw. In fact, I've taken a couple weeks off. My vacation time has built up, and there's not much goin' on this time of year."

"Tell me about it. With the snow still down so low -- it's below two thousand feet, you know, Blowout Road is still closed -- nobody's logging yet at all." Earl operated logging equipment for one of the larger logging companies in the area, Redd & Co. "Guess we better enjoy these Saturdays while we can, though. Once the season starts we'll be up there seven days a week till the snow falls again."

"I'm glad to hear you're not too busy now, Earl. I was hoping you'd give me a hand with something."

"Name it, Warren. You fixing your roof? Hauling wood? Repainting your place?"

"No, nothing like that. I got myself tangled up in a mess over in Milford. Do you know Alice Lewis?"

"Sure. Her mother, Anna Swetzer, and my mom were always great pals. They went to school together, and later they were both in the Milford Women's Improvement Club together. Mom was a hostess and Alice Lewis -- her name was still Swetzer then -- was parliamentarian. They'd meet every other week, you know the sort of thing. What Did Santa Claus Bring, Humorous Anecdotes Of President Lincoln, that kind of stuff. I remember Mom teasing Alice about all the talks she used to give on 'Decorum, Deportment And

Development,' although it seems to me like a fair topic for a parliamentarian."

"Is that right? I didn't know your Mom was from Milford."

"Oh, she's not. She's only lived there fifty-one years. She was born in Salem."

Warren smiled. At that rate he could live in Campton for the rest of his life -- which he fully intended to do -- and never be "from" there. "Then you must have heard something about the Milford Bank Robbery."

"Good lord yes! We heard about nothing but that for months, right after it happened. I haven't thought about it in years, though. What in Sam Hill does that have to do with you?"

Reaching down on the seat beside him, Warren produced Monty's journal, a fat composition notebook, and a thin volume on the history of Linnton and Milford. "It's got an awful lot to do with me at the moment. Remember the fellow who was convicted of robbing the bank and killing the teller? Monty Lewis?" Earl nodded and Warren continued. "He did his time and was released from the federal penitentiary a few weeks ago. His life sentence was commuted to thirty years for good behavior."

"No kidding! That's a long time to spend in the pen. He had it coming, though."

"Seems that way. But his wife doesn't think so."

"Naturally. Rough spot for her to be in. But as I recall, the case against Lewis was really airtight. No loose ends."

Warren flipped through his notebook. "True, Earl. I wish I didn't agree. Unfortunately, Alice asked for my help, and I told her I'd do what I could."

"Help with what?"

73

"You didn't hear? Monty Lewis disappeared three days ago."

Monty's eyebrows rose. "Skipped town, huh?"

"Looks like it," Warren said. "But why? He's paid his dues. He has nothing to fear that way. After thirty years he gets to go home. Why just chuck it all and take off?"

"Beats me. Couldn't face people, maybe?"

Frowning, Warren started reading out items from his notebook, bits and pieces he had copied laboriously from Gabe's walls and ceilings.

October '34. BANK ROBBERY AND MURDER IN MILFORD. Two men, their faces hidden behind bandanas, robbed the Milford Bank on Tuesday. They burst in the front door and held everyone at bay at gunpoint. One of the gunmen forced an employee to open the vault, from whence the robbers took several bags, presumably of currency, and a large strongbox. During a brief scuffle one of the robbers was struck by a teller, Barney Pritchart, with a brass paperweight. The injured man fled, but at the door he turned and fired a single shot, killing Pritchart. A witness distinctly saw blood trickling down the robber's face, although the actual injury inflicted by Pritchart was hidden by the hat worn low over the man's forehead. Dr. Golden was summoned from Linnton to tend Pritchart, but by the time the doctor arrived the bullet had got the best of the brave man, and he died on the premises. Witnesses described the man who shot Pritchart as about 5'11", slender and with a slight limp in his left leg. The other robber was heavier set and about the same height. No better descriptions were given due to the hats and bandanas worn by the criminals to obscure their features.

Warren stopped for a sip of water. "And blah, blah, so on and so forth."

"Nothing new there, Warren. It took them a while to get on to Monty, didn't it? Seems like there was something bizarre that came up." The ranger nodded.

"A couple of the witnesses swore up and down that the killer was Monty Lewis; same height, same build, same limp. Couldn't see his face too clearly, of course, but what was visible apparently looked an awful lot like Monty. That was the one who got hit by Pritchart. All the same, nobody else could believe Monty was involved. It was unusual that he wasn't at work that day, but as there was a flu epidemic making the rounds of Milford just then, the manager didn't think too much of it."

Earl pondered. "But there was something else out of kilter. Monty wasn't really sick, was he?"

"Not with the flu, anyway. This is where it gets weird. When the sheriff went to the Lewis place to talk to Monty, there wasn't any Monty there. As far as Alice knew, he had gone to some kind of bank deal in Portland. Well, that looked bad for Monty. But even at that most of the folks in town couldn't believe it of him. He'd never given any trouble before, been a good worker when he could get work. He got behind on his land taxes once or twice, but he paid those off by working on the new county road, spreading gravel and what-not. How could a man like that rob a bank and kill a neighbor?"

Warren consulted his notes again. "Blah, blah ...

Four hundred thirty nine dollars in cash taken, plus a strongbox that contained the entire deposit ($62,000) of the United Northwest Railroad Company. The strongbox had been placed in the bank vault only a week before the robbery by UNRC President, our own Gilbert Callahan. The event attracted considerable attention at the time. The deposit represented the entire capital raised by Mr. Callahan in his latest round of financing for the troubled railroad. With that money, the final leg of the railroad was to be built, connecting Milford and Linnton with towns as far away as Sweetbriar Flat and Yellow Creek. Mr. Callahan left immediately after making the deposit on an extended trip to line up labor for next spring's construction season, and cannot be reached for comment. Several of the investors whose money was in the strongbox, however, did hear of the robbery. It is understood that there will be a substantial reward for recovery of the lost property and information leading to the conviction of those involved. Many local people have already begun their own searches for the lost money, and for traces of the criminals. The official manhunt and investigation continues as well. Memorial services for Mr. Pritchart will be held Sunday at the meeting hall of the Loyal Legion Of Loggers & Lumberman, Milford.

Kate interrupted Warren's recital to hawk some butterscotch pie, and made two sales. Earl passed a hand across his chin, trying to recollect every scrap of information, gossip or guesswork he had heard about the sensation of the decade.

"Monty disappeared for a few days back in '34, it seems like. That's what was so weird -- he turned up again, right in town, bold as brass. Is that why you're dragging all this up? Because you think his two disappearances are connected?"

Sighing, Warren spread his hands in the air.

"Alice thinks so. Apparently when Monty got out he had a bee in his bonnet about finding the 'real' criminals. He always denied it, you know. When he first turned up, after the robbery, he had an absolutely wild story about having been kidnapped, drugged, held for a while in some shack in the mountains, and then released near town. He claims they grabbed him on his way to work one day -- it turned out to be the day of the robbery, of course, but he didn't know that at the time, or so he says. According to Monty there were two guys who grabbed him, but he only saw one of them, and that only for a second. He threw in a few details for effect; said the shack was made of green logs -- small pine, he thought, and it had a woodstove in it. That he noticed the stove because when he first woke up his face was darn near up against it, and supposedly he had fallen on top of it when they first brought him in -- said it was cold so he didn't get burnt, but that's how he explained that cut on his forehead, which the witnesses said matched how Pritchart had hit that one crook. Monty didn't seem to be hurt when he wandered into town after the robbery, other than that cut and some bruises on his face. When he was first picked up, Monty seemed to be in such a daze that he didn't notice the cut. And later, when he got his wits back, he just kept repeating that he'd fallen against the stove -- actually, that he'd been pushed and fell against it."

"And the bruise on the cheek? That doesn't seem to be tied to the robbery," Earl put in. "What'd he have to say about that?"

"That he started mouthing off to his kidnappers, and they got fed up with it and let him have it with the butt of a pistol. He even specified that it was a forty-five caliber, and that they hit him so hard they

77

knocked loose his new gold tooth, which he later almost choked on and then spit out. Monty said he didn't remember much of anything after that; groggy all the time and didn't even have any idea of how long he'd been gone."

"But that's the craziest story I every heard. You'd think that if he was gonna come back, he'd have a better tale than that to tell. Otherwise, why come back at all? It's almost enough to make you think he was telling the truth," Earl concluded.

"Except that there was so much else against him. The witnesses, for example, who identified him. And the injury to his temple. How'd he get that if not in the bank? It's true there was no percentage in him coming back that way, but he clearly wasn't in his right mind when he did come back. The sheriff, and I guess the jury too, figured he must have got hurt, taken a hit in the head, after the robbery. Some thought he might have been double-crossed by his partner. The partner was never found, by the way. Or maybe that knock from Pritchart was enough to make him punch-drunk. Anyhow, he got hit, addled, wound up back in town. End of story. The jury brought in a conviction in half an hour." Warren closed his notebook.

"And the money was never found? Nobody claimed the reward?"

"Nope. There was an intensive search for days afterward, and the locals hunted on and off for years. Never found a thing." Warren shifted and stretched. "I suppose people are still looking for that loot. But it must be long gone, along with Monty's mysterious partner. Speaking of which," Warren put Monty's journal on the table and pointed out the last entry, of a few days earlier. "What do you make of this?"

Earl puzzled over it for a minute. "You think the partner's back in town?"

"Who knows? All I know for sure is that Monty's gone and Alice wants me to find him."

"So how can I help?"

"I've got an idea. Old Gabe Hanks isn't as off-the-beam as he looks, and he knows the mountains around Linnton better than just about anybody else."

"So?" Earl was plainly skeptical of any contribution from Gabe. "So, he didn't buy that little stove he's got in his cabin. He found it, out in the middle of nowhere halfway up Coffin Mountain. Small but in good shape, he said. And get this, Earl. He found it in the spring of '35!"

"You lost me, Warren. Who cares about his stove?"

"Look at it this way. Gabe finds a stove in the middle of nowhere, not even near a road, let alone a house. What's it doing there? Monty says he's taken to a cabin in the middle of nowhere, and there's a stove. Now, the newspapers don't say so, but my guess is it must have been an awful small stove; they'd of had to pack it in by mule or horse. Gabe remembers to the square foot where he found his stove, and it tallies pretty close with what Monty said about where his kidnappers took him. I mean, he didn't have any kind of precise idea, but he had a general idea of the direction, and said it was definitely uphill all the way, and he knew about how long it took to get there. That's all in the trial transcript. Trouble was, they knocked him out when they first grabbed him and he was unconscious for a little while, so he doesn't really know where they started from. That could be why the search teams could never find this cabin, and decided it was a figment of Monty's imagination. But if we proceed on the assumption that Gabe's stove is Monty's stove, we don't need to know where they started from. We'll just follow Gabe's directions."

Gloomily, Earl considered the probable reliability of Gabe's directions. "But suppose we do find the cabin -- well, really, the remains of a cabin. There won't be much left after all this time. But suppose we do? I rather doubt that Monty's been dragged off there again."

"Right. But I don't think we're going to find out what happened to Monty three days ago if we don't figure out what happened to him thirty years ago. I can't say that Alice has me convinced that Monty was innocent, but I don't see any other way of starting. And the snow line is above this spot now, so it'll be a nice hike."

"Is Jake the Wonder Dog going with us?"

"Good idea. I'll swing by and pick him up, then meet you at your place. Oh, and Earl --"

"Yeh?"

"Let's keep this to ourselves, okay?"

14

The pickup climbed slowly up the winding dirt road, Warren guiding it carefully around hairpin turns and up steep straightaways. Earl had traded places with Warren's motley hound, Jake, so that the dog could ride with his nose out the window without leaning heavily across the other passenger. Once or twice Earl turned the tables and leaned across Jake to get a better view of the mountain slope dropping sharply away, not a foot from the tires of the pickup. Although he was used to such roads, Earl couldn't refrain from peering out the window occasionally, a worried look on his face.

"Not much shoulder out there," he advised the driver.

Smiling half-heartedly, Warren said "Don't worry, Earl. The road's fine. Good and solid."

Earl didn't look entirely convinced. "I hope you're not just going by what Gabe said. Has anybody been up here after the winter? How do we know part of the road hasn't washed out, or slid down the mountain? We wouldn't have a snowball's chance in hell of turning around up here. You'd have to back up for ten miles."

Both men jumped as Jake let out a bark that reverberated in the cab of the truck and sounded like a miniature bomb going off.

"Holy -- what in God's name was that for?" Earl demanded in an injured tone. "I bumped my head on the roof."

Warren pointed up the slope to his left, just as a flash of grey darted into the trees from a small meadow.

"Wolverine. Jake must have caught the scent."

Jake's interest seemed to have been exhausted, however. He removed his nose from the window and settled comfortably against Earl, who gave him a dirty look and an elbow in the ribs.

Before long the woods of Douglas Fir around them thinned and finally gave way to meadow. Warren steered the pickup off the road and onto the wiry alpine grass. "This is the easiest spot to get up Coffin from. The road keeps going, but bends on around toward Sweetbriar Flats and then heads down. This is the best place to start hiking."

"Right." Earl stirred, reached over and unlatched the door, and nudged Jake out. Jake landed on the ground with a thud and leisurely began exploring the new territory, sniffing here, marking there.

Warren maneuvered his tall frame from behind the wheel and stood for a moment surveying the scene. Below him the meadow sloped away to the treeline. Above him -- he had to crane his sore neck to see it -- rose the rest of Coffin Mountain, above the steeply mounting grass, which even after winter retained some green. Patches of snow stood out in a few spots, but for the most part the southern exposure and lack of trees had rendered the ground bare and the going easy. Even the crown of Coffin Mountain, lower than those logged by Redd & Co., was relatively free from snow on this side. Up close, the mountain top looked rough and unformed, bearing no resemblance to its deceptively level appearance when seen from afar.

Earl was struggling into the straps of a rucksack. "What'd you put in here, Warren? No matter which way I arrange it there's always something sharp poking me in the back. And it's heavy, too."

"I'll take it, Earl. I brought along a folding shovel, just in case we need to poke around some. And also a scintillator. That's probably what you feel. It's all corners, and sharp ones at that."

"No, I'll take it. You just tell me what a scintillator is. I assume it scintillates, but that doesn't tell me much."

"You know, a scintillator. You swing it back and forth above the ground, and whenever it's above metal it gives off a certain noise. It can pick up stuff up to a foot underground. I thought it might come in handy, since we're searching for what's left of an old cabin. They must have used nails to build it."

"No kidding? That's pretty clever. Never heard of such a thing." Earl looked at the backpack with less resentment. "Maybe we'll find something, after all. And we have Jake's nose, too."

A tail wagged momentarily, and they set off up the slope that rose so steeply it gained a thousand feet in elevation in about a mile of walking. The air was cold and thin, and soon both men were panting. Only Jake seemed unaffected, dashing this way and that and covering about four times as much distance in his perambulations. The day was stunningly clear, rendering vivid and sharp the blue above, the green with spots of white at their feet.

They toiled upward in silence for some time, Warren leading the way. Once he stopped to consult a scrap of paper he fished from a pocket, then continued on. After about half an hour Earl called a halt by dropping abruptly on to his rear and stretching his legs out in front of him, pointing them downhill and digging his heels in against the mountain's pull. Only then did he spare any breath for conversation.

"Do you actually know what you're doing, Mister Ranger?" He patted his pockets to locate something, and pulled out a chocolate bar. "Want some?"

Before answering, Warren also sat down heavily, reached for the chocolate and broke off a chunk, and chewed it appreciatively.

"Believe it or not, I do. I had my doubts for a while. Gabe told me where to park and what direction to follow from there. But after that there wasn't much to go on except he said eventually we'd hit a big stretch of bedrock coming up through the grass. Not high, he said, you have to be pretty close before you notice it. So we must be pretty close, because I just spotted it before you dropped." Warren pointed. There above them was a spreading blotch of gray displacing the green. "We're almost there."

"Then what?"

"Then, once on the bedrock you head west a few hundred yards and the slope flattens out a bit into a small plateau. Gabe said it's the only flat on the whole southern side of Coffin -- that's easy enough to believe -- so we can't mistake it."

Earl digested that along with his chocolate. "If he's right about the flat, then it's encouraging. That would be a good place, maybe the only place, to build a cabin."

Nodding, Warren said, "That occurred to me, too. Maybe we are on the right track. Come on, let me take the pack now."

"You persuaded me." Earl gladly shrugged out of the rucksack and gave it to Warren. "I think the outline of your fancy machine is permanently imbedded in my back." At the movement around him, Jake got to his feet and trotted ahead, his cohorts trailing behind.

With their destination in sight, the two men utilized some of their energy for talking. "Another thing Gabe told me about," Warren began. "It's not connected to this business, mind you, but it's interesting all the same. He said about thirty years ago a forest fire swept through these parts, covered about ten thousand acres. Wiped out most of the woods altogether, except for one spot on the north side of Coffin Mountain. Instead of burning the trees black like usual, the fire just kind of skirted this one big stand of trees, didn't really burn them at all. But the heat was enough to kill them, and make them lose their bark, without turning them black. Gabe said the trees are still standing, no leaves, no bark, but all the limbs intact; and the trunks have weathered to a light grey. There's a whole forest like that, he says. The old-timers call it the ghost forest."

"I'll be darned. Never heard of anything like that. I'll bet you dollars to doughnuts it's just another tall tale of his."

"Could be. I wouldn't mind checking it out sometime, though."

Earl shook his head, which gesture was lost on Warren's back. "No thank you. Not today. One side of a mountain is enough for now. Say, here's the bedrock."

The three travellers slowed and looked around. Again referring to his notes, Warren pointed left. "Gabe says -- oh, look, he's right. You can see the flat from here. Just to the west there."

Following Warren's lead, Earl gazed west. The side of the mountain cut in suddenly, as if someone had sliced a large chunk off it, at the bottom of which was a small, even area, bordered on the downhill side by a tall, jagged outcropping of rock. Dubiously, Earl nodded. "That must be it, alright. It doesn't look big enough for a cabin, though."

Excited now, Warren strode forward. "Sure it is. That is, for a small one. In fact, apparently Monty always referred to it as a shack, not a cabin. It was probably just one little tiny room. That's all they'd need for shelter and warmth, and one small stove would be plenty to heat it. They'd just have to pack the wood a half mile or so, not bad at all."

They crossed the remaining distance quickly, with Jake frisking ahead. Propelled by eagerness, Warren reached the flat first, swung his pack off and rapidly assembled the scintillator. Earl watched curiously. The gadget that emerged looked like a rectangular metal box with a long narrow pipe emerging from one end, that terminated in a flat circular head. "That really works, huh?" he asked.

"Let's hope so." Warren fiddled with knobs and switches. "I haven't actually used it before. In fact, I just borrowed it this morning from Stan Nevil. But he said he's found all sorts of things with it: square-headed nails, old coins, even a piece of jewelry that his wife had lost in the garden."

"Hmmp. I'll believe it when I see it," Earl muttered. He watched closely as Warren painstakingly swept the head in wide, even arcs across the flat. A strange clicking noise came from the box, and a needle on the front wavered at one end of a gauge. "Is that what it's supposed to sound like? Sounds like a dead battery that doesn't want to be jump- started."

Warren frowned at him. "Shhh. I have to listen. Stan said the noise changes when you hit paydirt; the clicks get louder and closer together, or something. Turn into kind of a high hum."

Earl retreated to the edge of the flat, and made himself as comfortable as he could. Jake plopped down beside him, cocking his head from side to side and raising an ear at the unaccustomed noise. An osprey circled high in the air above them, visible against the light in the sky only when he banked to turn; his whitish breast made him invisible to the fish he preyed on until his swoop was already complete and he could flap away, clutching a squirming trout in his claws. Earl wondered idly whether there was a lake nearby. He fingered the grass around him, and cut his finger on its harsh blades. Suddenly remembering the wolverine they had glimpsed earlier, he put a protective hand on Jake and looked around uneasily. They hadn't seen the slightest sign of humanity in hours.

"Any luck, Warren?"

Morosely, Warren waved the question away. Then he stepped alertly toward Earl. "I know! We should test this thing on metal we know about. You must have something metal on you, a watch or snaps or something."

"Of course. The buttons on my shirt are metal, and my jacket has a metal zipper up the front."

Warren ran the peculiar device through the air above Earl, and it emitted a sharp howling sound. So did Jake.

"Good lord!" exclaimed Earl, as he scooted away. "Is that safe?"

Jake backed hurriedly away, keeping his eyes on the strange gutteral creature.

Too intent to be sidetracked, Warren returned to his search of the flat. "I gather that means it's working. There must be something here, a nail, a spoon, a bullet casing. Stan says it picks up even the tiniest objects."

Patiently, Earl and Jake watched the ranger cover the ground, twice, three times, four times. Finally Warren came and sat down beside them. By this time Earl was stretched out flat on his back, drowsily examining the sky line. "Ready to give up?"

Gloomily Warren nodded. "Doesn't seem to be much choice. If there ever was a shack here, there's nothing of it left to find. The wooden parts would have rotted years ago, and there sure doesn't seem to be any metal. Man, that is a blow, though. I can't think of anything to do next."

Earl let the strained silence last for a few moments, then said, "I can."

Surprised, Warren faced him. "Shoot! I'm listening."

"Well," Earl grunted as he raised himself to a sitting position. "Let's assume Monty's crazy story is true, and somebody did kidnap him. That's what you've done, right?"

Warren agreed. "So? Get on with it."

"Okay. If that's so, the kidnappers went to alot of trouble to make Monty out a liar. They obviously wouldn't want anyone to believe him. Therefore they wouldn't want to leave any tracks."

"Naturally," said Warren, a bit impatiently. "But what are you driving at?"

Placidly, Earl continued. "They could guess that somebody would look for them and their shack to verify Monty's story, so they wouldn't just leave it sitting around, waiting to be found. They'd get rid of it. And how do you get rid of a shack? Why, you burn it, of course, and cover up the burnt spot. And," Earl noticed the growing irritation on Warren's face, and speeded up his monologue. "And, you wouldn't leave a wood stove just sitting in the ashes. Now would you?"

"I see what you mean!" Warren's shout provoked a glare from Jake, who had been enjoying a short snooze. "You'd move the stove. But that means," he added, sadly, "that even though we know where Gabe found the stove, we haven't got a clue where the shack itself was."

"Not so fast, Warren." Earl waggled a finger at him. "Granted they'd want to move the stove, why move it here? Do you think they'd pack that little monster uphill if they didn't have to? Course not. They'd --"

"Dump it downhill!" Warren finished for him.

"Exactly. And take a gander above you."

Warren did so. He saw the line of Coffin Mountain's ragged top not a quarter of a mile up.

"And," Earl continued triumphantly, "why would the stove end up just here, of all places? What would happen if they just gave it a heave over the edge of Coffin?"

Warren swerved and pointed. "It would be stopped by the rock at the edge of this flat. Earl, you're a genius. The shack must have been right up on top of

Coffin, and they just heaved the stove over the side and burnt the shack! I'd bet my bottom dollar on it."

"Why guess about it? It won't take long to find out." This time Earl led the way, anxious to put his theory to the test.

With their energy renewed, the trio reached the top of the mountain in no time. So rough and uneven did it appear at this range, that no one standing there would have guessed it was the same mountain famous for its flat top. One end of the plateau rose considerably. Boulders were strewn about, and there were odd, isolated stands of stunted pine trees scattered around. Snow lay more heavily under the trees. Earl crossed the width of the plateau -- only a matter of some hundred yards -- and looked down into deep drifts of snow on the cold northern face of the mountain. Warren, however, made a beeline for the site directly above the lower flat and began clicking about with the scintillator, which he had carried in his hand from below. Almost immediately the noise changed to a hum, less than the howl produced by Earl's buttons but definitely something other than the indifferent clicking of before.

"I've got something, Earl! Where's the shovel?" Without waiting for a response, Warren got down on his knees and began scrabbling in the hard dirt. He picked up a small rock and started scraping at the topsoil.

"A nail!" he proclaimed, as Earl hastened up with the shovel in his hand. "It's a nail, Earl! Rusty but definitely nailish. And look, it's square, not round. Square nails haven't been made in a long time. This must be the place." He grabbed the scintillator again and excitedly waved it back and forth. Another hum rewarded him.

"I'll get this one!" Earl said quickly. He, too, kneeled and scraped with the shovel nose across the windswept earth. Not even the hardy, coarse grass of the meadow could take hold here, and he had no trouble in extracting another nail. "Keep at it, Warren. I think we're onto something!"

The ranger needed no urging. His manipulations of the scintillator resulted in an almost continual humming and an occasional howl from the machine. "Here's another nail! And a shotgun shell! And a nail!"

After sniffing the first few finds, Jake sat at the edge of the activity with a bored look on his face.

After about twenty minutes of frantic searching, reason asserted itself. The men raised themselves, rather stiffly, to standing positions. Earl rubbed a knee. "Think I must have landed on a rock."

Warren smiled ruefully. "Guess we got carried away a little. But this is great. I'd say it pretty much proves that there was a structure here of some kind. That's already a beginning. If only we could find something that links this to Monty, though."

"No reason to quit trying so soon. We've still got a couple hours of daylight."

Gratefully, Warren slapped Earl on the shoulder. "I like your attitude. Let's keep at it. How many nails could it take to hold together one little shack?"

One hundred and eighty four nails and ninety minutes later, Earl sighed and said, "Does that answer your question? To be honest with you, I'd just as soon not see another nail in my life. My knees are sore and my back is killing me." Jake was snoring contentedly.

Warren groaned in agreement. "Believe you me, I know exactly how you feel. You take a break, and I'll just make a couple more sweeps with this. Our rate of nail-discovery has definitely slowed over the last ten or fifteen minutes. We must have got most of them by now."

It took Earl several seconds to straighten himself. He put both hands on his lower back and rubbed. "Yow. I'll feel this for a while. Think I'll stretch my legs a bit."

Hardly noticing his absence, Warren continued the hunt. For the one hundred eighty fifth, and sixth, and seventh times the scintillator hummed. Warren threw the nails aside in disgust. Then a gleam caught his attention, and he bent forward till his nose almost touched the ground. His fingers scuttled forward and gently brushed away some dirt. The object glittered in the sun, like a small nugget.

"Gold?" Warren mumbled. "Hardly likely up here. Never any mines in this neck of the woods." Gently he picked it up. "Hey, Earl! Come take a look at this!"

Earl appeared from a stand of trees and walked up. He peered at what lay in the palm of Warren's hand, then gingerly lifted it. "Looks like gold, doesn't it? Not a nugget, exactly, though. It's pretty well polished, isn't it? Seems to have been worked. It's shaped a particular way, kind of like -- oh my God!"

"Yep, that's what I thought of, too. It's a gold tooth!" A thought niggled at the back of Warren's mind, a flitting recollection. Then he remembered. Monty had a gold tooth put in a few weeks before the robbery.

15

Sunday morning Warren awoke to gentle but insistent nuzzling from Jake. Opening his eyes, he squinted out the window and saw it was another dazzling day. Surprised to see that he had slept until 8:30, an uncommonly late hour for him, Warren understood Jake's impatience: breakfast was overdue. His quick movement out of bed reminded him suddenly and painfully of the previous day's adventure, but with his soreness was anticipation and curiosity. If he could only verify that the bit of gold from Coffin Mountain was in fact Monty's tooth, it would lend some credence to Monty's wild story and cast a new light on his recent disappearance. From a phone call to Alice Lewis last night, Warren had already learned that Monty, like almost everybody else in Milford, used old Doc Golden to take care of dental problems.

While cooking breakfast -- apple dumplings with last year's dried winter apples, and strong black coffee, with a bowl of something meaty for Jake -- the ranger reviewed his notes on the newspaper accounts of the robbery, paying special attention to the appearance of Monty on the scene. He also dug out his new county map, but soon put it aside. Restless before the appointment he had made with Dr. Golden, Jr. at noon, he decided to pay a visit to the Linnton Free Library to satisfy his inquisitive mind on a few other points. Grabbing his green Forest Service jacket with the national forest emblem on the sleeve, Warren opened the kitchen door and Jake dashed out, eager to investigate the new day. They climbed companionably into the pickup and headed for Linnton.

The Linnton Free Library was in an ornate old brick building with columns in front holding up a peaked porch roof, rare in those parts. It housed not only the library but also the Linnton Town Registry, in which the drama and messiness of local life was reduced to neat, precise data: births, deaths, marriages, taxes paid and taxes due, land bought and sold, lawsuits filed, verdicts won and lost, town expenditures and receipts, and all the other details of municipal interest that both reflect and overlook so much of small-town life. It was to the Registry Office that Warren went on his arrival in Linnton.

The door was locked, but on it was posted the home address and phone number of the Registry Clerk, one Virginia Gustave. Her home was very near the Library, and Warren walked the few blocks with Jake at his heels. Just as they swung open the small wrought-iron gate in front of the house, the door opened and a young woman appeared, turned out in her Sunday best. She looked at the tall man at the gate with friendly curiosity.

"What can I do for you?" she greeted them. "No, wait. Let me guess. Your fiancee's getting impatient and you can't wait till tomorrow for a marriage license." She giggled and Warren decided he liked this impertinent young lady.

"Not quite, no," he smiled in return. "My name's Warren Ascott. I was hoping --"

"A dog license, then," his inquisitor interrupted. Her shoulder-length blonde hair gleamed in the sun that slanted toward the door. She held out her hand and Jake happily frisked up to be petted.

"Not that either. Actually --"

Again he was cut off. "I've got it! Your wife just had a baby and you've come to file the certificate. You were pacing in frenzied worry all night, chain-smoking and tearing at your hair, and now you're so happy and relieved to have son and heir that you totally forgot it was Sunday and the Registry's closed."

She grinned. "By the way, I'm Virginia Gustave. I assume that's who you're after -- this morning, I mean."

By now Jake had sensed the beginning of a beautiful new friendship, and was lying with his front paws on Virginia's feet.

"Jake, come here," Warren commanded, to distract this girl's rather intimidating attention from his uncertainty on how to receive her remarks. They did sound a bit forward, but -- He decided they just expressed her native friendliness and good nature, and responded in kind. Jake ignored him and continued to gaze up at his new friend.

"Wrong on all counts, Miss Gustave. No fiancee, no wife, no baby. A dog, yes, but he already has a license. What I'm really after is information."

The clerk pulled her feet out from under Jake's rather heavy paws, and started down the sidewalk toward Warren. "Well, Mr. Ascott, you've come to the right place but at the wrong time. I was just on my way to church. Perhaps you'd care to escort me?"

This caught Warren off guard. "Well, now that you mention it, I'm not really much of a lad for the services. I'm more the church-on-Easter-and-Christmas type myself. Can't seem to stay awake through the sermon. Nothing personal against the preacher, of course; just a constitutional infirmity of mine."

"I see. This business of yours, is it very pressing?"

"Oh, yes. The pressingest. And it's an awfully fine day to spend in a dank old church."

Virginia considered. "The church is no danker than the Registry Office. Howsomeever, I suppose I could be persuaded to forego the Right Reverend Ferguson for once. I don't think my soul's in any immediate danger." She presented an elbow for the ranger to take. "Not yet, anyway."

"Not ever, I'm sure, Ms. Gustave," Warren responded gallantly. "Not when you do such nice things for people as go to work on Sunday."

They fell in step naturally, with Jake treading almost on Virginia's heels, and Warren forgot his sore muscles. He explained what he was looking for, which prompted a flood of questions interrupted only by her production of a large metal key. The questions resumed as soon as they had stepped inside, and before long the clerk had wormed a full explanation out of Warren: what he wanted, why he wanted it, what his interest in Monty's disappearance was.

"Lewis, Lewis," the young woman mused. "I know I've come across that name recently somehow."

"You probably read about Monty in the newspapers when he was released last week," the ranger suggested.

The blonde hair rippled as she shook her head. "No, it was something here in the office. A birth, maybe? Or taxes? Oh, I know. A land transaction. Some Lewises bought the haunted house in Milford. We cover the whole county here, you know."

"Run that by me again," Warren directed, plainly skeptical.

Stung by his disbelief, Virginia said frigidly, "I don't chew my cabbage twice. Look for yourself." She opened a drawer from among dozens of drawers of identical appearance without even glancing at the contents list on the front, and riffled through the index cards inside with a practiced hand. She couldn't have held the job for many years considering her youth, but she certainly conveyed an impression of efficiency. Noticing Warren's admiring look, she rightly took it as a tribute to her work.

"I practically grew up here. My aunt was clerk for thirty-two years and I'd stop off on my way home from school and spend a couple hours here each day. I'd help her with her work -- that's how I got to know everything in this office inside out and backwards -- then she'd give me a lift home. Fair trade, I always figured. Let's see, seller to buyer index, no, buyer from seller index, hmmm... Here we go Landry, Latham, Lingeford -- too far. Okay, here it is. 'Lewis, Montgomery, and Lewis, Alice, wife of same...'" Virginia pulled a heavy volume from a set on shelves behind the index files, and thumbed through the pages. "Yep, here it is." She thrust the book toward her guest and pointed out a particular deed. Warren looked with interest at the document.

"That's the location, alright. 'To be held in fee simple absolute' -- whatever that is -- 'by the said grantees Montgomery Lewis and Alice Lewis his wife, as long as the grass grows and the rivers run...' That ought to cover it. Oh, wait, 'or until such time as they convey said fee,' and so on and so forth. It doesn't say anything here about things that go bump in the night."

"No, it wouldn't, would it? That house had been on the market for ages. They wanted to find buyers, not drive them off. Strictly speaking, though, the house isn't haunted. It's cursed."

Warren laughed. "I guess these fine distinctions escape me. What's the difference?"

"Obviously, a haunted house has ghosts in it. No ghosts here. Just a curse that makes everyone who lives there go insane or die a horrible death. Your friends should have checked it out better before they bought," Virginia stated with finality.

"But you don't really believe all that, Miss Gustave? That's child's talk."

"Shows what you know, Mr. Ranger. It's not only me that believes it. It's a known fact. Here. Read this."

From yet another stand of drawers, Virginia produced what seemed to be a scrapbook, and flourished it before Warren. He laid it on the worn oak desk, pulled up a chair, and leafed through it. Page after page was taken up with newspaper accounts, letters and scrawled notes about the Lewis house, then called the Crossburn Mansion. The entries dated from 1921 to 1938, and painted a picture of supernatural gloom. Two different, unrelated families had resided in the house between those years, and nearly every member of both families either died a premature death, or lived to old age in a state of insanity.

"I told you so," Virginia couldn't resist saying.

"But where is all this from? Chances are it's just some kook who was obsessed with the house."

"In a pig's eye!" the clerk responded indignantly. "It was my aunt who put together that scrapbook, and a saner woman you never will meet. She only did it because other folks were always bringing this stuff to her. A lot of people thought there should be a record of it, kind of official- like. You have to admit, it's all pretty weird."

Weird indeed. Warren agreed with that assessment. If the reports were accurate, no one in the house escaped the "curse," over the course of seventeen years. Even the family dog developed a glassy stare and the staggers, and died before its time. Resolutely he put the book aside and said scornfully, "I don't believe a word of it. Let's get on with more important things." All the same, his thoughts kept returning to the house.

"Fine by me." Virginia seemed miffed. "Where do you want to start?"

Sensing the need to placate, Warren shrugged his shoulders. "I wouldn't know where to begin. I'm trying to see what became of some of the people involved in the robbery or the investigation or the bank back in '34. Like did any of them leave town after the robbery, or start living a better life, in terms of material goods -- any noticeable change in any of them?"

Virginia sighed. "That's a tall order. Well, as far as having more money, we could check the tax lists. That would also show real estate taxes, so we might be able to pick out anybody who gained or lost property. As far as moving away, we don't really keep track of that. You'd just have to notice if their names stopped appearing on the tax or voting lists or something."

For the next hour and a half, the two of them pored over dusty books and ledgers and lists, while Jake lay patiently by the door. Finally Warren straightened up and said excitedly, "It looks to me like somebody did skip town not long after the robbery. At least, he'd been paying taxes regular as rain for years before that, but there's no mention of any tax payment for '35. It's Gil Callahan. As I recall he wasn't directly connected with the bank, but I'm sure he was mentioned in the papers somehow."

Virginia set down the thick book she had been examining and rubbed her wrists.

"Don't jump the gun here. We may find him in here." She quickly located a tome entitled 'DEATHS: MILFORD' and placed it on the desk, shoving other volumes aside to make room for it. "You say he paid his taxes in '34 but not '35? Uh-huh, this explains it." She pointed out a death certificate in the name of Gilbert Callahan. Warren peered at it.

"This lists the cause of death as unknown. Didn't they even make an educated guess in those days? It doesn't give the date of death, either. That space is left blank."

Looking over the ranger's shoulder, and briefly admiring it as she did so, Virginia said, "They weren't too picky about things like that back then, but this looks pretty skimpy even so. It's signed by Doctor Golden, that would be the father of the present Doctor Golden. But he's dead now, too, so I don't suppose that helps much."

Warren considered this. "Maybe yes, maybe no. I'll be seeing the good doctor in about ten minutes. He said on the phone that most of his father's files are still stored in their attic. Apparently neither generation believes in throwing things out, especially patient records. This may not lead us anywhere, but it's enough to make me want to know more."

"In ten minutes?" Virginia looked meaningfully at her watch. "It sounds as though you'll be skipping lunch."

Warren nodded. "Seems as though." He waited while she let them out of the office and locked the door behind them, and he noticed again how her hair shone in the spring light. "But perhaps," he continued, slightly stiffly, "we could both find time for lunch next Sunday. I understand there's a respectable diner here in town. After church, of course."

Virginia accepted with a smile. "Don't spend too much time in the Lewis house, then. I wouldn't want you howling at the moon or anything if I'm going to be seen with you."

16

Warren peered into Doc Golden's waiting room, temporarily blind in the relatively gloomy interior after the thin but bright sunlight outside. Why are doctor's offices never sunny, he wondered as he settled himself into one of the hard, straight-backed chairs. The doctor poked his head out of the examining room at the sound of the front door closing, and nodded to the ranger.

"Be with you in a minute, Warren. Just have to give one last injection," and he waved the syringe in his hand, as if to explain it further. No further explanation was needed, as Warren was as familiar as anybody else in town with the doctor's predilection for giving shots. Pills seemed to be quite outside the scope of the Golden practice; whether in for a cold, a cut or a sprained ankle, the patient rarely escaped the doctor's syringe. In a minute the examining-room door opened again, and a young boy scuttled down the corridor.

"Don't you forget to come back day after tomorrow," Doc Golden's voice pursued the boy.

"Fat chance!" Warren heard the victim mutter as he increased his velocity toward the door.

Jovially the doctor shook Warren's hand and led him up the corridor.

"So there's something I can do for you, is there, with those old records of Dad's? Say, come to think of it, I haven't seen you here for quite a while, Ranger. What's your vaccination record look like? We're smack dab in the middle of a little epidemic of measles now. I'll bet you could use a booster shot."

Firmly, Warren said, "Forget it, Doc. I had the measles when I was twelve. I've also had the chickenpox, the mumps and strep throat, so just put that right out of your mind."

"Tetanus?" the doctor ventured hopefully.

"No shots, doc. I'm here for information only. Specifically, information on Gil Callahan and Monty Lewis. I know you're supposed to keep your mouth shut about your patients, but Callahan's been dead for thirty years, and Monty's wife gave me the go-ahead to look at his records, so I think we're all set."

"I reckon so," Doc Golden agreed. "No skin off my nose if you want to see a dead man's file, and if Alice wants you poking around about Monty, I'm in favor of it, too. She's the salt of the earth as far as I'm concerned." He pointed to the stairs, which prominently occupied the end of the corridor, and said, "The old records are up there. Help yourself. They're not alphabetized, but they are grouped by year. With just the few hundred people Dad had to draw from as patients, it shouldn't take you too long to find what you want. Here, I'll go up with you a minute to get you started. Say, you know your grandmother was about the only one around here who never went to him."

"I didn't know that. Who did she go to?" Warren was surprised, since Doc Golden, Sr. had no competition in town during his grandmother's time. He walked through the door held open for him, and surveyed the stacks of cardboard file-storage boxes, each with the years covered neatly labelled on the front.

"Nobody. Didn't trust doctors -- she wouldn't go to one to save her soul. Not that a doctor would be much help for that," the second Dr. Golden mused. "Dad told me about it. At one time there were lots like her, but she held out her whole life." He mumbled to himself as he scanned the labels. "1942-43, '44-45, must be over this way ..."

"That's right!" Warren exclaimed. "I remember now. Whenever she had an ailment she'd treat it with some God- awful smelly stuff --"

"Asafetida it was," the doctor interjected. "People used to carry it in a little bitty bag around their necks all winter long. Thought it cured everything from arthritis to toothache. Personally, I'd rather put up with a toothache than that smell."

"Amen!" the ranger agreed emphatically, waving his hand in front of his nose as if the smell had wafted down the years. "Which way did you say the mid 1930s would be?"

Smiling at some dusty memory, the doctor shifted a pile of boxes and squeezed behind it. "Your guess is as good as mine. I'll check this part and you try over by the window. Your grandmother was really something. Stoic, you know. Real pioneer stock."

Warren nodded. "Yup. She chopped her own firewood right up to the end. Even when she was in her seventies. Speaking of firewood, her husband -- not my grandfather, but her first husband -- was quite a character, too. Once somebody was stealing his firewood, after he'd got it all bucked and split and stacked, so he decided to fix their wagon but good. So --" Here the ranger interrupted his story to sneeze violently from the dust stirred up from moving boxes, "-- so he hollowed out some holes in a couple of those nice chunks of wood, stuck in a little blasting powder in each one, and put 'em back up on the woodpile."

Chuckling, Doc Golden turned to announce he'd discovered the nineteen thirties. "What happened? Don't tell me he forgot and burned those logs himself."

"Hardly. A few nights later old man Pritchart (you know, Barney's father) got up with a bang -- found his stove door blown clean off and the stove pipe every which way. Nobody ever bothered the firewood again."

"Crude but effective, I guess." The doctor grunted as he lifted a box from the floor to a bench near the window, then removed the cover and started flipping through old file folders. "Think we're in the right time frame, here, Warren. We ought to find both Monty and Gil in here."

"I sure appreciate your help, Doc. Nothing against your father, but I'd need an interpreter to read these things."

"It's not so bad when you get used to it. In fact, I've got more appointments coming up pretty soon, so you'll be on your own soon. Look, see that thing there?"

Bending closer, the ranger squinted. "I see it but I don't recognize it. Is it a medical symbol?"

"Naw. It's an 'H'."

"An 'H'? As in horse?"

"Well, actually, as in hepatitis, but it doesn't really matter. You just need to recognize it when you see it. And that little squiggle there is a 'Y'."

"You're kidding."

"Not at all. Next time you see it, you'll know it. And there's an 'E' and a 'T'. You'll figure it out." Doc Golden smiled reassuringly. "By the way, your grandmother sewed herself up once. Did you know that?"

"Come again, Doc. You lost me."

"Well, I told you she didn't like doctors. One time, when she was home alone, way up the canyon there with nobody around for miles, she cut her thumb real bad with a butcher knife. In fact, she cut it clean to the bone. She could of just wrapped it and hopped the speeder into town, it was a straight downhill ride, wouldn't even have had to pump. But instead she chipped off some ice from something and laid that on the cut, then got out her sewing basket and calmly stitched up the cut. Good thing it was her left hand she hurt. Dad saw it a few weeks later, right before she took the stitches out. He said it was a beautiful job, healed as good as gold and no infection. Couldn't have done it better himself."

Warren shook his head in amazement. "Grandma always did pride herself on her small stitches, but that's a bit much!"

"That's what Dad thought, too. Many more like her and he wouldn't have had a practice. Hey, I found Monty's file! He had dental work done here that year, nothing else. A gold tooth. Must have been a good year money-wise for him. That was quite an investment back then."

Recalling Monty's journal entries, Warren nodded. "That was probably the best year he ever had. How detailed is the file? Could you match up the record with an actual tooth?"

"Hah. No way. We didn't make wax impressions or take x-rays back then. It just says here, 'Molar, gold, lower left.'"

Disappointed, Warren brought out the small lump of gold they had found on Coffin Mountain. "So you can't tell me whether this could be the one your dad describes there?"

Doc Golden inspected the item. "Oh, I can tell you that. It's a molar, alright. They're easy to recognize, shaped differently from the other teeth. Broader, for grinding, you know. What's more, this one is hardly worn at all. Must be new. Say, I'll be late for my next patient. You're on your own now." And he hastened down the stairs to the waiting room.

Warren stood quietly for a moment, watching the particles of dust dance in the sunlight. Afternoon peace pervaded the stuffy attic, and the shadows thrown by the musty boxes and trunks cloaked the room in mystery. "I'll be damned," murmured the ranger.

17

"So Monty was telling the truth!" Earl Millican exclaimed over the clatter of diners in Kate's cafe. "And that was the shack we found. Poor old Monty did all that time for a crime he didn't commit. How come Gabe didn't speak up at the trial about finding that damned stove?"

Ranger Ascott shrugged. "That's plain enough. He hadn't even found the stove then. It would still've been covered with snow. He found it the following summer, and didn't think to connect it up with the crime. No reason he should; it wasn't a big issue at the trial. Alice was the one who told me about Monty nearly falling on it. She was the only one who paid any attention to his story, because she was the only one who believed it."

Suddenly Kate appeared at their table to clear away the dishes from the special of the day, chicken-fried steak. Warren was relieved to see the remains disappear; the special wasn't sitting too comfortably in his stomach.

She interrupted their talk. "You fellows have to hear this. The Swenson boy just told me the cutest antidote."

Warren surreptitiously rubbed his stomach. "I could sure use a good antidote about now, Kate."

Earl smiled. "Tell us the anecdote, Kate. If it's from a Swenson, it must be corny."

"I guess it is, a bit. One Norwegian came up to another Norwegian and said, 'Hey, Olaf, I defended you the other day. Somebody said you weren't fit to eat with the dogs, and I said yes you were!'" Kate grinned and waited for the response.

"I fell out of my cradle laughing at that one, Kate," said Earl. "And what's more, I heard a Norwegian tell it about two Swedes."

"Don't let the Swensons hear you say that," Kate reprimanded him. "Mrs. Swenson hasn't been in a laughing mood since her daughter lost the Miss Dairy contest to that Johansen girl over in Sweetbriar Flat. She's got pretty darned uppity over it, too. Not Mrs. Swenson, I mean the Johansen girl. Well, need I say more?"

"No, no," Earl assured her.

"Definitely not," Warren added.

"Enough said," piped up a customer at the next table.

"Well, fine then." Kate swept away in a clatter of dishes. "You can get your own coffee, too. You know where the pot is."

"As you were saying, Warren," Earl returned to their earlier topic of conversation. "Alice isn't the only one who believes Monty's story now. But what do you make of Monty's disappearance? We know now that he hasn't skipped out."

"That worries me more than anything, Earl. He was kidnapped once, gets out of prison, then turns up missing straight away. You know, the money taken in the robbery was never found or accounted for."

Earl mulled this over for a minute. "You're thinking maybe Monty was kidnapped again by the same people. But that doesn't make sense. If he was innocent he wouldn't know anything about the money. He was the perfect fall guy. Why grab him again?"

"I can't figure it that way, either. Like you say, the real criminals would have no need of him now.

So I think Monty must have taken off to find them. In fact, I think one of them showed up in town here not long ago and Monty recognized him. That explains the recent entry in his journal. Monty must have taken off lickety-split to trail this guy in hopes of finding out what really happened."

Again Earl pondered it. "But why in blue blazes would this guy put in an appearance around here, just when Monty gets out of prison? That seems like a pretty tall coincidence. Unless Monty ..." Earl trailed off.

Sighing, Warren nodded. "I know what you're thinking. No one would bother to come back unless Monty had something they wanted, like the location of the money, for instance. That never was found, even though people hunted for years. The investors in Callahan's railroad, whose money was stolen from the bank, had a hefty reward up for a long time, but nobody ever collected it, and it wasn't from want of trying."

"That seems to bring us back full circle to Monty being guilty," Earl noted. "After all, his tooth up on Coffin could be explained by his being one of the conspirators. There was a falling out among the crooks, Monty got the short end of the stick, got hurt and dazed and then picked up by the sheriff. Just because his shack existed doesn't automatically mean the rest of his story was true."

"I grant you that, Earl, but why tell any of the truth at all if he was one of the thieves? And why would they leave him behind if he was the only one who knew where the money was? And if he wasn't the only one who knew, why would one of them pop up here when Monty is released? No, it just doesn't wash that way. What's more, I'm like Alice in that I can't believe it of Monty."

"I hate to pull the rug out from under your feet, Warren, but Monty was no angel. At least, local rumor had it that he was in on that dynamiting of the Jap boarding house back in '34. You ever hear about that?"

Casting his mind back to Monty's journal, Warren reluctantly conceded that he had.

Earl continued. "That was a dirty piece of business, if you ask me. If Lewis was so ready to blow up somebody else's house and chase people out of town by scaring the bejesus out of 'em, why would he turn up his nose at robbing a bank? Maybe he would draw the line at murder, but that probably wasn't planned; just a foul-up somewhere along the line."

"Beats me, Earl. I don't have all the answers yet by a long shot. But my gut instinct is that Monty is clean on this one. Okay, maybe it's just because I want to believe that, but that's how I'm looking at this whole thing." Warren reached down on the bench beside him and lugged up a heavy sheaf of papers bound loosely together with a faded red ribbon. "Here's the transcript of Monty's trial. I found out from Linch, Fowl & Crook, the law firm that handled Monty's defense, how to find it."

"You're pulling my leg!"

Warren assured him, "No, I mean it. That same firm is still in business. Different lawyers, of course, but the same firm. It's not that unusual to have a law firm that continues on from generation to --"

"Not that! Do you mean to tell me there really is a law firm called Linch, Fowl & Crook? If that doesn't inspire confidence!" Earl grinned.

"Be that as it may," Warren continued, somewhat severely, "they were very helpful with the transcript. Take a look at this." He pointed out a page which recorded part of the prosecutor's examination of one Miss Crossburn, proprietor of the small clothing store near the bank.

Q: And where were you the afternoon the bank was robbed?

A: I was in the bank writing up a deposit to my savings account.

Q: Did you see everything that happened during the holdup?

A: Yes. It was very hard not to.

Q: Can you identify any of the men who held up the bank?

A: The man who walked with a limp was Monty Lewis.

Q: Was he the man that shot Barney Pritchart?

[Pause]

Q: Speak up please, Miss Crossburn. Was he the man who shot Barney Pritchart?

A: Yes.

Q: Are you sure? Remember he wore a red handkerchief around his face.

A: I know, but I could see his eyes, and the build, and the same limp. Oh, it was him, alright.

Q: Thank you, Miss Crossburn. You may step down.

"Three other witnesses confirmed Miss Crossburn's identification," Warren explained. "Then, at ten o'clock the next morning, according to the transcript, the defense lawyer had his only defense witness take the stand: Monty Lewis."

Q: Now, Monty, I want you to tell the court in your own words where you were while the bank was being robbed. Take it slow and easy and describe to them what you told me.

A: Thursday night I worked pretty late at the bank and then stopped by the tavern next door for a beer or two. It was getting dark when I started for Haven. About half way a car cut in front of me and forced me to stop. Two men with masks over their faces jerked me from my car, punched me a couple of times and managed to tie my hands behind my back. One put a blindfold tightly around my eyes and loaded me in their car and drove off. I think the other one must have driven my car away. We drove two or three miles or so, and the fellow parked the car and we waited. After what seemed about half an hour, the other fellow joined us. "They won't find that car for a few days," I heard him tell the other.

Judge: Did you know where you were, Monty?

A: No, sir. I was blindfolded.

Judge: Go ahead then.

A: Well, we started walking up this trail for quite awhile. Once my blindfold slipped down and I caught a glimpse of a small creek the trail seemed to be following. One of them quickly tightened up my blindfold again and did a good job of it. That was the last thing I saw that night. After awhile the trail seemed to leave the creek and became very steep in places. I tumbled down several times due to being blindfolded. The falls were kinda hard on me -- with my hands tied behind my back I'd usually land on my face. I heard one of them say that we were only a few feet away then. I fell again when we got inside some shack that was there. That time I must have hit my head but good, because I didn't remember anything more until early the next morning.

Prosecutor: This is a very interesting story, but I see no proof that shows it's any more than that -- an interesting story.

Judge: I think Monty is entitled to try and prove he didn't rob the bank. After all, a person cannot be in two places at the same time. Continue, Monty. What happened when you came to the next morning?

"Then Monty talks about how he loses his temper and starts shouting at the kidnappers, calling them sons-of- whatnot, etc., and gets a smack in the face with the gun butt. Later they let him stumble out of the shack in the early morning darkness to answer nature's call, and later yet give him some whiskey." Again Warren referred to the transcript.

A: That whiskey must have had something in it, because I didn't remember anything until I woke up Saturday about noon. I was still in a daze and light-headed, but evidently I made it out to the Haven road because that's where the sheriff picked me up. That was the first I'd heard of a bank robbery.

Judge: Does the prosecutor have any question of Monty?

Prosecutor: No, your Honor, but if the defense rests I would like to call Alice Lewis to the stand as a rebuttal witness.

Judge: You may step down now Monty. Will Alice Lewis come up and be sworn in, please?

[The witness was sworn in.]

Q: Now, Alice, if Monty was missing from Thursday night until Saturday noon, why did you not report this to the police?

The transcript recorded Alice's testimony about Barney Pritchart calling from the bank to say he and Monty would be in Portland from Thursday night until some time Saturday; and that she knew where he was so he wasn't missing.

Q: But Mrs. Lewis, Barney Pritchart couldn't have made that call from the bank Thursday, because he wasn't working that day. And besides, we know he wasn't in Portland on Friday because [prosecutor turns and faces jury] he was working in the bank on Friday, the day it was robbed. We have his body to prove it.

Judge: Do you rest your case, Mr. Prosecutor?

Prosecutor: I do, your Honor.

Earl shoved the transcript back across the table.

"So what does that prove, Warren? We already knew the story Monty had cooked up."

"True, Earl, but I think this tells us two things. First, that either the good Miss Crossburn was perjuring herself like crazy," his choice of words reminded Warren of the "Crossburn curse" and the many cases of insanity in that family, and he hastened on, "or, we have a clue to the identity of the real robber. He must have looked one hell of alot like Monty himself, for everybody to be so sure of it."

"Except, of course, unless it was Monty himself," Earl put in gloomily.

"Well, right, except for that, of course. And the second point," Warren went on determinedly, "is that bit about Pritchart. I asked Alice about it, and she's dead sure it was him. She knew his voice, had spoken to him on the phone many times. So if Alice is telling the truth -- and we're assuming she is," here he glared at Earl, "then what was Pritchart doing at the bank that day, and without Monty?"

Shrugging, Earl said, "I give up, Ranger. What was Pritchart doing at the bank that day?"

"Pritchart was at that bank that day," Warren intoned, "because he was In On It."

18

"So what it boils down to is this," Alice summarized, her voice earnest and intense. "Pritchart purposely called me up so I wouldn't worry when Monty didn't turn up that day, so that he could be framed for the robbery! My God. So I played right into their hands by testifying about that."

Warren gently picked up her hand and squeezed it. "Don't do that to yourself, Alice. There's no way you could have guessed. What's more, things obviously didn't go according to Pritchart's plan. Don't forget, he was killed."

"I'm glad!" the words came out with such venom that the ranger was taken aback.

"Can't say that I blame you, Alice, but please don't dwell on that part of it. Look at it this way. Pritchart's death tells us quite a bit about what was going on. I mean, he was killed by one of the robbers. They were already turning on each other. Monty said two men kidnapped him. Now, assuming whoever organized this would want to keep to a minimum the number of people involved -- less risk and a bigger cut for each of them that way -- then it makes sense that Barney Pritchart was in on the kidnapping. That leaves one other kidnapper."

Pausing, Warren leaned back on the sofa, displacing the cat as he did so, and looked around the Lewis living room. The crisp sunniness of the recent weather was still holding, but didn't seem quite enough to overcome a vague gloominess in the room. The cat meowed plaintively and insinuated herself onto the ranger's lap, under his folded arms. Warren conceded to the point of giving the animal a token stroke on the head, eliciting a rumbling purr.

Alice stirred from her reverie. "Be that as it may," she leaned forward to refill her guest's glass with home - pressed apple cider, "it doesn't really get us anywhere, does it?"

"Not so fast. I think we can make a couple pretty sound conclusions from it. First off, we have to factor in this character who showed up when Monty was released. What's in it for him to hang around Haven? He must think Monty has or knows something he needs. Did anyone ever come snooping around, either recently or thirty years ago, like they were looking for something?"

Shaking her head, Alice said, "Never."

"No break-ins, searches, anything like that?"

"There was nothing, Warren," Alice said, a bit impatiently. "I can guarantee it."

"Alright. In that case, this joker must think Monty has some information."

Wide-eyed, Alice guessed, "The money!"

"Exactly. What else would he be after?"

"Hang on. That can't be it. Monty doesn't know anything about it."

Taking another drink of cider and stretching out his long legs, Warren responded, "That in itself tells us something. We know Monty's innocent." At that Warren firmly suppressed his doubts. "Judging by the way he turned up after Monty's release, though, this other fellow doesn't know that. Which means only one thing."

"Well, don't shilly-shally around," said Alice without even a pretense of patience. "What's it mean?"

"Why, that he was double-crossed, too! Get it? Pritchart gets involved, presumably for a share of the proceeds, and winds up dead as a door-nail. Definitely not what he had in mind when he started out on this little venture. Then this buddy of his shows up thirty years later, which must be because he's still after his share. He got shut out, too, although not killed in the bargain. Since Monty didn't do it, there must be a third person involved, who double-dealt both Pritchart and our new arrival. But," here Warren leaned forward in his intensity, and the cat let out a yowl and leaped onto the floor, tail twitching angrily. Before moving two steps, however, she flopped down, panting. "Your cat doesn't look too healthy," observed the ranger mildly.

"Forget the damned cat, Warren! Get to the point."

"Sorry. Didn't mean to keep you in suspense. The point is that this other fellow thinks Monty is the one who did the double-crossing, so he can't be the brains behind the whole shebang. And what's more, whoever did do the planning must have known a good bit about what went on in Haven and Milford. You mark my words, Alice," said Warren emphatically, "to find out who put together this whole shootin' match, we have to be looking pretty close to home."

Nodding in agreement, Alice said, "That all fits, and so does one other thing."

"What's that?"

"There's nobody in Haven or Milford or anywhere else roundabout who looks like my Monty. Now, every witness at that trial swore that the robber who killed Barney was Monty -- there must be some kind of resemblance between the two. So if this Mr. X who masterminded the whole thing is local, then it must be the other one who looks like Monty."

Glancing at Alice approvingly, Warren agreed. "And that's who's looking for Monty now, or else who Monty is looking for. So we have something to go on in our search for him. Plus, I have some ideas about this local contact, too, but I have to do some more research first."

"But, Warren," the loyal wife said hesitatingly, and fell silent.

Curious, the ranger urged her on.

"There is one little detail that doesn't make sense. If the boss of this whole thing is somebody from around here, why isn't the other guy, you know, Monty's look-alike, after him instead of Monty? He must be the one with the money."

Patiently Warren explained again. "Because, Alice, he doesn't know. He thinks Monty is the one who put the plan together. Although, now that you mention it ..." Warren's voice trailed off and he stared vacantly at a small and droopy apple tree in the yard.

"What? Although what?"

"Hm? Oh, nothing, yet. I just thought of something I should have done before. Tell me," he said, changing the subject rather abruptly, "why are your fruit trees doing so poorly? You always had such a green thumb."

Alice smiled wryly. "You tell me. Last spring I planted an apple tree and two plum trees near the house, one greengauge plums and one Italian prunes. I even watered them all through the last half of the summer, which was so dry for us, you know, but they look downright pitiful anyway."

"Maybe it's the Crossburn curse," Warren said lightly.

"Come again? The Crossburn curse?"

"You mean you never heard about it? You bought a house with a curse on it, that's why it went cheap. You wouldn't believe the number of people who take it seriously, too. The town clerk in Milford has a whole scrap book on it. Her aunt was a true believer," Warren continued. "She supposedly 'documented' every early death, case of insanity and what-have-you that happened here, all, of course, as a result of The Curse." He chuckled. "Maybe your fruit trees are the latest victims."

"Let's hope so, Warren," Alice said quietly.

"Whatever for?"

"Better them than Monty. Find him, Warren. Just find him."

19

The modern blandness of the Ranger Station was a welcome change after the dated atmosphere of the Lewis house, redolent (or haunted? Warren thought grimly) with past lives and present sorrows. Although he was on vacation, the ranger had come to his place of work and surprised his secretary, who had not dallied in taking advantage of his absence to reorganize Warren's files. Caught in the middle of her self-imposed task, she peered at her boss over a young mountain of file folders, manila envelopes, charts and aerial photographs of the national forest.

"Oh, Mr. Ascott! It's only Tuesday. You said you'd be gone till next week."

"It's nice to see you again, too, Miss Winley. I see everything is ship-shape while I'm away." He frowned good-naturedly at the mess.

"You're not exactly away now, are you?" she responded tartly. "It will be ship-shape by next week, and if you were where you're supposed to be now, it would be ship-shape now as far as you know. I mean, as you would know if you were where you're supposed to be."

"Are you trying to tell me that what I don't know won't hurt me? That may be true as a general rule." The ranger began sifting through one of the stacks of paper on his desk. "In this particular instance, however, I need very much to know what I don't know. Good lord, you've got me doing it. What I need to know is," he tried again, "where are the district maps for the north side of Coffin Mountain, and what are the earliest aerial photos we have of that area? Can you make even a wild guess where we might find them in this sea of paper?"

"I have not the slightest need to make a guess, wild or otherwise, Mr. Ascott." Miss Winley picked her way across the cluttered floor to a series of tubes leaning against the far wall. "Here are the district maps in geographical order starting with the southeast quadrant of the district and progressing in logical and orderly fashion to the northeast, northwest and southwest. Let me see. Coffin, Coffin ... Ah, Coffin Mountain, northern exposure. Exactly where it ought to be. Unlike some people I could name," she added under her breath. Extracting a map from the cardboard tube, she handed it primly to the ranger.

"Thank you, Miss Winley. I'm duly impressed. Now let's see what you can do with the photos."

"A simple matter." She made her way to a corner. "Arranged in reverse chronological order. Therefore the oldest photos would be at the back. The powers that be didn't authorize aerial photos until after the war. The earliest we have is from, let me see, 1950. Coffin Mountain, yes, north side, taken from Doublerock Mountain looking south. Is there anything else you need?"

"Only a spot to spread these out." Glancing at his desk, which was hidden under mounds of something or other, Warren smiled at his secretary. "You'll be relieved to know that I won't be in your way any longer. I'll take these home and go over them on my dining room table. After all, I am on vacation."

"And certainly living it on the wild side, too," she observed dryly.

* * *

Jake bounded up enthusiastically as the pickup pulled into the driveway. As soon as Warren opened the door, Jake thrust his large head inside and energetically sniffed at his master. "No secrets from you, huh pup? I confess, I was petting a cat today."

The companions entered the house, which still smelt of the red cedar from which it was constructed. Depositing his burden of maps and photos on the table, the ranger made straight for the kitchen to put together lunch for the two of them. Warren was entering that stage of bachelorhood in which occasional loneliness seemed a fair price to pay for domestic peace and routine. In short, he was getting set in his ways. He liked his two cups of coffee in the mornings, his hobby of wood carving in the spacious second-floor workroom, his walks and talks with Jake.

"Am I getting old?" he wondered aloud. Jake responded with a brief wag of his tail, but was clearly more interested in the culinary aspects of the immediate future.

"Fine, fine, here's your grub. Earl should be here soon, so don't take all day."

Few admonitions could have been less needed, as Jake swallowed the dish of food in three gulps.

With little wasted motion, Warren rummaged in the refrigerator and put together an appetizing meal from the previous night's roast beef, which he ate cold with a bottle of beer and half a loaf of sourdough bread. After clearing up the dishes from the small kitchen table, he stood by the living room window while he finished his beer, watching with appreciation the lively yet soothing bounds of the Little Bridge River in the foreground, with the town of Campton visible in the distance. Finally he sat down at the large table and began unrolling maps. So absorbed was Warren in this task that he was unaware of his visitor until Jake alerted him by issuing a startling woof and trotting to the front door.

"Earl, thanks for coming," said the ranger hospitably, opening the door. "Come in, take a load off."

"With pleasure. I've been on my feet all day. "My wife wanted me to clean out her sister's attic today, so I got a good early start. Cleared out boxes of stuff and put 'em all in the kitchen by the back door to get rid of later. Then she sees some of the odds and ends in the boxes, and starts in on me for throwing out such things. So then I had to take the durned junk back up!" Only after delivering this indictment of married life did Earl sit down.

"One man's trash is another man's -- or sister-in-law's -- treasure," his host commented.

"Basically," Earl concluded, "I'm damned if I do and I'm damned if I don't. But that's by the by. Incidentally, there was one interesting thing up in that attic: a huge old cistern. Seems like those were a pretty common feature of the old houses around here. Used 'em to collect rainwater from the roof and then they'd funnel it downstairs. Besides being an easy way to supply water to the indoor plumbing fixtures, rainwater was supposed to be good for the skin or the hair or the insides or some such nonsense. Pretty clever construction, though."

"Sounds like it," Warren responded, "but I'm more interested in the layout of Coffin Mountain at the moment." He pointed to the aerial photo that occupied most of the table top. "Take a gander at this. It's from 1950. Give you any ideas?"

Earl shrugged. "So it's Coffin Mountain. North side, I'd say."

"Correct. Now, here's a district map from the depression. There was a huge logging project that included the south side of Doublerock Mountain, which is just to the north here, and was supposed to include the north side of Coffin as well. As it happened, before they started cutting on Coffin a forest fire went through and burnt or scorched most of the project area, so they never bothered with it. Remember I told you about that ghost forest?"

Nodding, Earl replied. "Yeah, I remember, but I don't see what you're getting at."

"Well, that's the fire that produced the ghost forest. But the interesting thing is the roads that were built in expectation of logging Coffin. Of course, when I say 'road' I'm not talking superhighway. Enough trees were felled for a bulldozer to ram through and that's it. Not a road for driving on, but enough to skid the logs over. You can still see the traces of those roads on the photo taken a few years later, and there's only one that makes it to the top of Coffin instead of dead-ending in the middle of nowhere."

"I'm with you so far, Warren, but I still don't understand where we're heading."

Shuffling the papers around, Warren brought out a map of the larger area including Milford and Haven. "Here's Haven, where Monty lived. Here's Milford, where the robbery took place. This is about where Gabe Hanks' cabin would be. And that is more or less where we found the stove." He pointed to marks he had pencilled in on the map. "Think like a crook. You've planning to rob a bank, maybe planning to kill someone. The bank is in a narrow canyon bounded on one side by a river. No escape there. Only one road out of either end of the canyon, easy to block. You'll be between the devil and the deep blue sea. What do you do?"

"Get a horse!"

"Exactly. Which is what they did, according to the newspaper accounts. But check out this photo again. All along here," Warren sketched an imaginary line with his finger, "the timber is too thick even for horses. And in this direction," again he indicated, "you could ride for weeks and never hit civilization. So what's a poor robber to do?"

"I gotta hand it to you, Warren. You do know how to think like a criminal," said his friend admiringly.

"Thanks. I'll take that as a compliment. But you see what I'm driving at. The only reasonable escape route is right up the north side of Coffin Mountain, across the top, then down the other side into Sweetbriar Basin and the whole network of trails and roads over there. Easy as pie for anybody who knows the land, and it wouldn't be more than a few days ride."

The men were excitedly tracing this hypothetical ride when the phone rang. Warren left the room to answer it, and Earl could hear little of the conversation. In a minute the ranger returned to the living room, practically at a run.

"What's up, Warren?"

"That was Alice Lewis. The police just found a body near the old shake mill outside Milford. They called Alice because she had reported a missing person. She's supposed to go look at the body and see if it's Monty."

20

Alice sat quietly in the front seat between Warren and Earl, seemingly oblivious to the chuck holes in the road that sent them all swaying from time to time. Soon they reached the smoother county road leading to Milford, and Warren increased his speed. The beauty of the drive was entirely lost on all of them.

The pickup sped through Milford and onto the shake mill grounds just out of town. Two cars were already there, and half a dozen official-looking individuals wandered or stood about, and stared curiously at the newcomers. Sheriff Grinder was on the spot to open the door and help Alice out as soon as the wheels stopped turning.

"Hello, Earl. Here, Alice, let me give you a hand," the sheriff said politely.

Without even glancing at the sheriff, Alice jumped out of the cab of the pickup and walked with quick but firm steps to where Doctor Golden, Jr. stood beside a form on the ground. Some effort had been made to cover it with a tarp, but an indefinable quality in its shape identified it unmistakably as a human body.

The doctor stepped forward. "Alice, this is not Monty. These state troopers are fools. Idiots. If they all had half a brain they'd be half-witted. I told them that I've known Monty for years, seen him as a patient most of his life so I've seen more of him than most anybody else, and this was not him, but that wasn't good enough for 'em. They had to hear it from you. It isn't him, I guarantee it. They have approximately a thimbleful of brains all put together. If you combined their intellect you might, if you're lucky, come up with --"

"Stow it, doc, that's enough. We need an identification from a family member," one of the troopers broke in testily. "This Lewis fellow is the only person been reported missing around here in months, and this one here," he indicated the corpse with the toe of his shiny black boot, "sure fills the bill as far as our description goes. When you got here as examining post-mortem physician and told us it wasn't him, we tried to get hold of Mrs. Lewis but she'd already left her house, at least there was no --"

Disgusted, Earl Millican broke in. "For God's sake, get on with it! If Doc Golden says it ain't Monty, then it ain't. Let Alice take a look and put her mind at rest, then we can get her out of here."

There was a general movement and scuffling of feet at this, and one of the troopers removed the tarp. The small mill building in the background, long unused and rickety in the extreme, cast a sharply-defined shadow over the small group of people and stole away the warmth of the sun. Escorted by both Earl and Warren, with the doctor hovering protectively nearby, Alice approached the corpse and glanced at it, then started back, suddenly pale. Warren and Earl fell back with her, then moved forward again with her, like back-up dancers behind their leader. Alice fixed her eyes on the body and forced herself to view the face steadily.

"That is not my husband," she said calmly. "For a second I thought it was. The resemblance is remarkable. But it isn't Monty."

She turned coolly and walked back to the pickup. "Shall we go, Warren?"

"Sure, Alice," the ranger answered gently. "Are you okay?"

"Quite alright. I'm sorry about that poor man. I'd like to go home."

Holding out the pickup keys, Warren said to Earl, "Would you mind driving Alice home? Maybe you could find someone to come stay with Alice for a day or two, too," he added in a low voice. "And Doc," he said, turning, "I need a favor. If you'd ride with Alice and Earl --"

"Only too glad to stay with Alice," the doctor responded promptly, "I'll tell you what. I'll take these two home in my car, and you'll be free to ramble around on your own," he continued with a shrewd glance into the ranger's face. "Don't worry about Alice. I'll see to her."

"Thanks. Before you go, though," he asked as Earl conducted Alice to the doctor's car, "what can you tell me about his death?"

The medical man shrugged. "Not much to tell. Blow to the back of the head, with considerable force judging by the wound. Can't say what did the job exactly; something with at least one sharp corner, though, I'd bet. The post-mortem will tell us more."

"When did it happen?"

"Best I can do is to say sometime yesterday, probably morning. At least twenty-four hours ago. Yes, Warren" the doctor added, anticipating the next question. "I'll keep you posted."

By the time the doctor's car had disappeared from view, Warren was deep in conversation with Sheriff Grinder. "Warren, you know I shoot straight with you. We don't have a durned thing on this yahoo. No wallet on him, no i.d. of any kind. Between you and me, I think that's why these ..." He jerked his thumb toward the state police, "were so eager to get Alice out here. They'd a been in hog heaven getting it wrapped up so fast. Without it being Monty, they don't have a clue to who that is, let alone who'd want to do him in."

"Are they sure it wasn't an accident?"

Sheriff Grinder grunted. "They're not sure of anything, but they won't admit it. But due to the damage on the back of the head, the force of the blow, they're not ruling out homicide."

"Force of the blow? Sounds pretty vengeful."

Overhearing this last remark, the trooper who seemed to be in charge and still smarting from Doctor Golden's remark and the general lack of respect for their methods, interjected, "Gee, that's an astute observation, Ranger. Wouldn't ever have occurred to us, of course. But now that you mention it, it does raise the question of who would have been so, so ... annoyed, shall we say, with this poor guy. Here he is, a stranger in town, turned up from nowhere within a day or two of the time your buddy Monty Lewis disappeared so mysteriously. I just wonder if the two could be connected, don't you?"

"Get off it, Sergeant," said Warren angrily. "Just because a man turns up missing doesn't mean he's out to murder somebody. What possible connection could there be between the two?" He asked the question with considerably more bravado than he felt, since he had already been speculating about precisely such a connection since his talk with Alice that morning.

"All I know is," the officer said stubbornly, "something happens out in the boondocks here once in a blue moon, and all of a sudden we have one man getting killed and another man dropping out of sight. Hard to write off as a coincidence. Not to mention the trivial little fact that the missing man has already done thirty years for, gosh oh golly, what was that little scrape he got himself into? Wasn't it, why yes, I think it was -- murder! Isn't that right, Officer?" He turned to his subordinate for confirmation of his sarcasm. "No, I don't suppose Mr. Monty Lewis would stoop to hitting somebody over the head. Course, I wouldn't put it past him to shoot somebody, but heaven forbid we might think he'd hit somebody over the head."

"I don't have time for this," Warren observed, half to himself, and strode to his pickup. The ghostly, deserted mill receded within the frame of his rearview mirror as he pulled away. "Damn you, Monty!" he muttered. "For an innocent man, you do the guiltiest things."

21

The flank of Coffin Mountain rose up steeply behind Gabe Hanks' cabin. The pounding of Warren's fist on the front door was audible not only in the cabin, but in the surrounding clearing as it reverberated off the dense stand of trees around it. "Gabe! Come on out here!" Warren shouted. "I need some information quick, and I'm willing to pay for it." To this there was a responsive shuffling from behind the cabin, and Gabe appeared around the corner.

"I like the sound of that, Ranger, 'deed I do. Care for a sip a somethin'?" As on Warren's previous visit, the old man had a jar ready to hand.

"Absolutely not." Warren said it with conviction. "I don't have time for socializing, Gabe. This is strictly business." Mentally he added, "And not until hell freezes over am I going to taste that again."

Slowly advancing, the strange old man motioned his guest inside. "I don't spend much time inside in these fine days, but I reckon whatever you're after we'll find on my walls, ain't that true, Ranger?" Gabe chuckled in his gaspy, echoing way and followed Warren inside.

"You're a step ahead of me, Gabe. You don't even seem surprised to see me here."

"Naw. I knew you'd be payin' me another call before long. You didn't ask all the right questions the first time around, did you? Heh, heh." Hanks looked craftily at his visitor and swung his arm broadly, in a gesture that took in the walls around them and the ceiling above. "Lotta information in them papers, but we was nobody's dummies back them. That so-called reporter for the *Standard* didn't know Jack Shit about what-all went on in town."

Seating himself, Warren tried to look casual. "Like what, for instance?"

"F'rinstance, I got lots a f'rinstances, Ranger," said Gabe, emitting that chuckle, which was already getting on Warren's nerves. "I recollect, howsomever, that you mentioned payment."

Warren suddenly realized that Gabe was cradling Molly in his hands. "Hello, Molly. Payment. What did you have in mind?"

"Oh, no, Ranger. What did you have in mind? There, there, girl. Ol' Gabe's takin' care of you."

"Hm. Let's say I know of a good three cords of wood, already split, that I could get a certain mill owner to part with."

"Say away, Ranger, but that don't cut no ice with me. I got a whole forest full of free wood right outside my door."

"Not already split."

Not bothering even to answer this, Gabe shrugged indifferently.

"Then let's say," Warren paused and hastily surveyed the room, his eyes lighting on the ubiquitous

Mason jar. "Let's say I have a case of real Kentucky whiskey with your name on it."

Gabe's eyes lit up, and Warren knew he had made a sale. "Now let's talk."

Lolling back in his home-made chair, Gabe rolled his eyes upward as if searching for inspiration from heaven.

"Ain't always been just Swedes and Norwegians hereabouts," he began. "Was a time when some Japs came to work, way back in the Depression. Brillo brought 'em in 'cause they'd work cheaper." He paused, and Warren stifled the urge to shake him. "You like ol' Monty Lewis, don't you, Ranger?"

"I just want it straight, Gabe. Don't doctor it up for me."

"Heh. I wasn't aimin' to. It just so happened that those Japs lived in a boardinghouse in Milford. And one fine day ..."

Warren sighed. "I know all about that, Gabe. Somebody blew the boarding house to kingdom come, and Monty was in on it."

"Yup. Monty, and Tobe Tobias, and Gil Callahan, and a few others."

"Hm. I didn't know Tobias was in on it."

"Oh, sure. Here's how it happened." Gabe recited, in full detail, the whole drunken escapade. "And there's something else I'll bet you don't know."

"What?" Warren demanded impatiently.

Mechanically searching near the chair, Gabe's hand came into contact with his reliable jar, and he took a long swallow. "Abner Brillo, dog that he was, was pretty friendly with the woman who ran that boarding house."

"For cryin' out loud, Gabe, I don't care about who slept with who in Milford thirty years ago."

"Mebbe, mebbe not," commented Gabe. "But you might be interested to know that she was so friendly, she gave Abner quite a bit of storage space in that house free of charge. Ol' Brillo kept all sorts of records there: deposit records, vault inventories, employee records, bank audits. Thought you'd like that," said Gabe, closely observing the ranger's face.

"Mebbe, mebbe not," Warren quoted. "What else?"

Grunting slightly, Gabe hoisted himself out of his chair after setting Molly carefully on the floor. He lounged carelessly around the room, stopping to squint now and then at his unique wallpaper. Finally he stopped in front of an issue from mid-1934, and placed a scrawny fingertip against a front-page article entitled "Local Man Receives Recognition In Banking World." Warren hastened up and began reading.

> A new railroad venture has received a nod from the banking establishment in San Francisco. The head of the investment portfolios for Bank Western, one of the largest San Francisco banks, has recommended to its clients investment in the project of one of Milford's own, none other than Tobe Tobias, mill owner, railroad financier, and all-around entrepreneur. Milford should be proud to have a businessman of Mr. Tobias' caliber. The article went on to describe the various stages of the railroad and its anticipated completion date, capability and profits.

"I admit I didn't know that," said Warren, "but what makes you think I'd be interested in it? And why would the *Standard* reporter know any more about this than anything else that went on?"

"I don't say that he did, Warren, nor that he didn't," retorted Gabe rather cryptically. "What I'm sayin' is that Tobe got a real big kick out of that article. Drank a few toasts to the durned fool who wrote it, that's what I'm saying. He seemed to find it a damned fine joke."

The ranger pondered this for a while. Eventually Gabe continued. "That's what I know, and it's all I know, Ranger. Don't know what it means, or who really killed ol' Pritchart, one of the worst and most popular poker players ever to infest this canyon. If you can make sense of it, fine with me, if not, fine with me too. But either way you owe me a case of good Kentucky whiskey. The real stuff," he added wistfully, eyeing his jar.

"Sure, Gabe. You'll get it." Warren asked the old man a few more questions, then made his way back to the highway.

* * *

When the ranger arrived home, Jake was not the only one there to greet him. Doctor Golden was sitting on the front steps.

"Hi, Doc. What brings you here?"

"Alice got a strange phone call right before I left. She doesn't know about it yet, because I didn't want her being harassed by those chowder-headed cops so I answered the phone every time it rang. This call was from her bank. They wanted authorization to wire some money from her and Monty's savings account."

"Where to? And who to? And why?"

"Don't know why, or who. All they knew was that they got a call from the Western Union wanting a guarantee for payment of three hundred dollars. San Francisco office."

"San Francisco? What is he up to now?" Warren wondered aloud.

Dr. Golden asked "What is who up to?"

"Monty, of course. He's the one in San Francisco. And I think I know why."

22

Only a few leaves were out, but the narrow canyon was wrapped in green thanks to the Doug fir trees that made up most of the forest. Warren Ascott rolled down the window of his pickup in spite of the chill of the morning, and sniffed appreciatively at the scented air that wafted in. After just two days in San Francisco he felt like he'd been away a week, and decided that the roughness in the road was a small price to pay for being the only one on it -- infinitely better than the well-tended but nerve-wracking thoroughfares of San Francisco. His drive from the airport in Salem had been pleasant enough, but as he approached Haven he drove with unaccustomed speed to Alice Lewis' house. Before the ranger's pickup rounded the corner nearest her house Jake, who had been left there for the duration of his master's absence, had pricked up his ears and was whining expectantly at the front door. Alice noticed, and was standing on the front porch when he came into view.

Warren waved through the open window as he parked, then unfolded his long legs from behind the wheel and stepped out.

"Hello, Alice, and howdy Jake!" He grunted softly as Jake welcomed him with two paws on his chest. "Alright already! Down." Jake subsided and allowed the ranger to give Alice a quick hug.

"Don't get your hopes up too high, Alice. I didn't find Monty, yet, but it's starting to look like we can unravel this whole mess after all, and unless I miss my guess he'll turn up soon, and in one piece to boot."

Leading him past the scrawny trees and scraggly grass of the garden into the living room, Alice sat him down on the sofa in front of which, on a small table, was a tray laden with coffee and sandwiches.

"Well?" she said expectantly. "Oh." As an afterthought she shoved the tray closer to him. "Help yourself. I thought you might be hungry after the trip. What did you find out? And what led you to San Francisco?"

"I guess you could say a boardinghouse, a railroad and a newspaper led me there; not to mention a death certificate and a broken leg." He picked up a ham sandwich in one hand and a steaming cup of coffee in the other. "Thanks. This'll hit the spot."

Politely Alice waited for her friend to chew a few bites, then resumed her questions. "Don't be so damned mysterious, Warren. What makes you think Monty is okay?"

"Because he needed money. He contacted your bank to get some out of your joint savings account." The ranger tactfully omitted Doc Golden's censorship of Alice's phone calls, and saw that she was too excited about Monty's safety to wonder how he got information from the bank. "And he only wanted three hundred dollars, which is quite a sum, but not enough to indicate he was in a real jam. Just enough to get by on for a bit while he's on the road, pay for a hotel room, get some decent food, that sort of thing."

Nodding her agreement, Alice said, "That makes sense. But why was he there in the first place? And also, oh, Warren, you know the police think he killed that guy out at the shake mill. If he does come back ... maybe it is better if he's out of sight for a while."

"Definitely not," he responded firmly "That only makes things worse. Especially since I think he must have been there when that fellow was killed."

133

"What?" Alice said, shocked. "Warren, how could you say that?"

Warren raised a hand placatingly while he finished swallowing. "Hold your horses, now Alice. Don't get me wrong. I don't think Monty killed the man. But he must have talked to him. I found out some things that led me to San Francisco, but there's no way Monty could have known them. Yet he ended up in the same place. Why? Don't forget he took off in the first place right after he first saw the face of the fellow who's now dead."

"The journal entry!" Alice exclaimed.

"Sure the journal entry. That's the face he could never forget -- his own, practically. It wouldn't be hard to track down a stranger around here. They must have had it out, somehow, and Monty got some information out of him, and that's what took him to Frisco."

Mulling this over, Alice frowned in concentration. "But who did kill ... Good God! Warren, that man must have been killed by the mastermind -- the third man, the local one -- remember, we talked about him before! Pritchart was one of the gang, and this man who looked like Monty," Alice rushed on with her thoughts, "he must have been the one who shot Pritchart in the bank, and now he came looking for the money and he's dead, so --" she stopped as she saw Warren shaking his head.

"Nope. That third man couldn't have killed this guy four days ago," Warren said with certainty.

"Why on earth not? It fits perfectly!"

"Except for one detail. He's dead too."

* * *

After talking to Alice for almost an hour more, Warren loaded Jake, his cedar dog bed and a few leftover cans of dog food into the pickup and headed for the Millican home. As at most homes in the area, the back door was used by almost everyone who came to the house, and thus the ranger was escorted through the kitchen and past the still-warm evergreen-berry tarts on the table. Earl grabbed one as they passed.

"Take one, Warren. What are you waiting for, an engraved invitation?"

Needing no further urging, Warren followed suit and ate not one but two tarts appreciatively. "Tell your wife these are great."

"I won't. She already knows it, and thinks she's spoiling me as it is. Don't want to give her any encouragement in that kind of thinking."

They sat down in the Millicans' shabby but inviting front room. "Glad I caught you at home, Earl," said the ranger. "Thought there might be some logging starting up somewhere by now."

"Not yet, but not much longer. The lower elevations are already opened up, but my outfit is supposed to cruise some of the upper units before anything else, so we're still sitting on our duffs for a while yet."

"Bad for you, good for me. I could use your help again." Warren paused to consider his phrasing, but Earl guessed his intentions.

"Not another trip up Coffin Mountain? Christ on a crutch! I'm still sore from the last time," he complained, rubbing his knee tentatively as if refreshing his memory on his grievances. "My back, my knees, my ... oh, jeez, alright. I suppose you have a good reason."

Confidently Warren said, "Only the best, and it's not all the way up the mountain this time, either." He proceeded to relate all he had discovered since their last talk.

Earl listened attentively, but shook his head in puzzlement when Warren finished. "So what you're telling me is that we have to find the money that was taken in the robbery, and that'll clear Monty, and you know where it is."

"I didn't quite say that, Earl."

"You distinctly said, Warren," Earl quoted, "that we have to find that strongbox, and that it would clear Monty, and that you know where it is."

Agreeably, the ranger nodded. "That's what I said."

"So why did you say you didn't say it? Do you or do you not know where that box it is, and will it or will it not clear Monty?"

"I do know where it is, and it will clear Monty."

"Alright then. Why in hell you say it, then say you didn't say it, then say it again is beyond me, but if that's what needs doing then let's do it. Talk about making a federal case out of something. Criminy!" Earl continued muttering for a minute as he prowled the house looking for boots, jacket and other paraphernalia needed for a hike in the mountains. As he rummaged in the kitchen for a chocolate bar to take, he fortified himself with another berry tart.

"By the by, Earl," Warren said casually, "you might dig out a rucksack, too."

Groaning dramatically, Earl ventured, "Not that scintillator again!" Seeing Warren's grin, he continued, "At least you could have the decency to file those corners down. Or better yet," and he grinned back, "carry the damned thing yourself!"

The two men were loading their gear into the ranger's pickup, with the help of Jake who was managing to entwine himself amongst the human legs around him and causing a few curses, when the sheriff's car stopped in front of the house and Ron Grinder came up.

"Alice said I might find you here, Warren," he said. "Got some news."

"Spit it out, Sheriff. From the tone of your voice it isn't good news."

"Good and bad, really. Monty Lewis is back in town. Turned up at home about an hour ago."

Exchanging a quick glance with Earl, Warren said, "So far so good. What are you going to ruin it with?"

"Well, it didn't take the state cops long to catch up with him once he got there. They were going to pick him up for questioning on that body at the mill. Only thing is, when they showed up he disappeared again. Skedaddled out the back and headed for the hills, with his old thirty-ot six hunting rifle. The cops put out an all-points bulletin on him as armed and dangerous. Some of the locals are getting scared and reporting sightings of him. Looks like he's heading for Coffin Mountain."

23

"Alice must be frantic," Earl commented as they sped by her house.

"Most likely, but we can't stop to see her now. I'm guessing that Monty -- damned fool that he is -- is smart enough to lose himself in the woods for a while. I s'pose that's why he grabbed the rifle. But if they close in on him, thinking he's murdered twice already and knowing he's got that gun, something tells me he won't live to tell the tale. I just hope his running off buys us enough time." Warren spoke grimly, and Earl glanced at his set face.

Fingering the pile of papers Warren had thrust in his lap, Earl asked, "Is there anything I can be doing right now?"

Warren replied, "I have a pretty good idea of the spot we need, but take a look at that aerial photo there, see where I've marked?"

After a short struggle to unfold the large document and spread it out without interfering with the driver's vision, Earl grunted. "Hmp. I see it. Seems to be about two miles off the highway, on one of those old logging cuts we were going over the other day on that old map."

"Right. Try and locate some kind of landmark so we know where to park and leave ourselves the shortest distance to cover on foot."

Scanning the photo for a few minutes, Earl said, "Got it. Pull over at that bend in the Little Bridge River where there's solid bedrock beside the road. You know the place, where the salmon hang in the pool to rest before jumping the rocks right up above it."

"Good. From there we follow the logging cut for a couple miles until we hit the rock face at the foot of Coffin's northern side. Doc Golden described the spot pretty well in his report."

"Doc Golden? Did he tell you about this place when you were over there the other day?"

"Wrong Doc Golden. I mean Senior, the old man. He wrote all about it thirty years, no, make that twenty-nine years ago."

"I'll be jiggered!" Earl exclaimed. "But how --" Catching a glimpse of the ranger's face, he restrained his curiosity. "At least tell me this, Warren. How are we going to recognize this old logging road? It was grown over pretty good in that picture from 1950, and that was a long time ago. It must be a regular jungle by now."

"We'll know it when we see it. Remember, they didn't actually log the area, so the road itself should be grown over by trees that are thirty years old, much younger than the old-growth on both sides of it. If I can't tell the difference between 'em I'm not fit to be a ranger." So saying, he lapsed into silence that lasted until they reached the river bend and began unloading their equipment.

Besides the scintillator and Earl's chocolate, they had a compass, the folding shovel, work gloves, and a large gunny sack. In addition Warren had folded and put in his pocket a paper covered with the handwriting of Dr. Golden, Sr., which Earl had scrutinized on the drive but couldn't begin to decipher.

Looming before them the woods seemed, to uninitiated eyes, to present an unbroken wall of indistinguishable trees. Casting only a brief look, however, Warren stepped into them, moving at a speedy but consistent pace. Earl followed dutifully. Conversation seemed somehow inappropriate on this trek, and the muted voices of the forest surrounded them: the wind stirring the boughs high overhead, the gurgle of the Little Bridge River receding gradually behind them and, occasionally, a sharper sound, as though the otherwise-silent footfall of an animal had clumsily displaced a rock. No birds lightened the air with their song, and only the smallest patches of sky dared peek through the living canopy above them. The going was easy and nearly noiseless on a thick carpet of fir needles that cushioned their steps and prevented hindering brush from growing up under the high-growing tree limbs.

Their progress was rapid and the slope not yet overly steep. Earl had provided himself with a small cushion between his back and the scintillator inside the rucksack, and could move forward with some degree of comfort. Nonetheless he felt tense and hurried, and sensed that Warren, too, was pressed by an urgency he didn't care to discuss. Again he heard the strange, rocky sound, but this time not so distant. For the first time since entering the woods he felt uneasy, and refrained from looking behind him only with considerable will power. It occurred to him to wonder why Monty had also chosen Coffin Mountain as his destination, which in turn prompted him to consider why he had gone to San Francisco, and what he had found out there, and even, finally, whether he and Warren were the only ones on their way to locate a large amount of lost money. With a major effort Earl repressed those morbid thoughts, and reassured himself that Monty was an innocent victim and not an armed killer. All the same, a vision of the body at the mill suddenly flashed before his eyes, and he stepped up his pace just a little.

They had continued on for about half an hour, without exchanging a single word, when Warren called a halt and surveyed their surroundings. For the first time, Earl noticed that Warren was holding a compass.

"We must be near the ledge now, Earl," said Warren, breaking his long silence.

"You could've fooled me. Looks just the same as when we started. But lead on, I'll follow." Adjusting the rucksack slightly, Earl observed the ranger puzzling over Dr. Golden's script. "Problems?"

Sighing, Warren answered, "No, I think we're still on the right track. If so, we'll be hitting the ledge in about four hundred yards."

Beyond the "road" the forest was so dense that four hundred yards was far beyond the range of visibility, so the men plunged forward in the direction indicated by Warren. Earl could hear a muttering from ahead, and realized that the ranger was counting off strides. Before long he heard a satisfied "Hah!", and hurried forward. Warren was smiling broadly and leaning against a rock ledge that soared some three hundred feet above them.

"I take it we're doing well, Ranger," said Earl.

"That's putting it mildly, Earl. We're sitting pretty. Old man Golden knew what he was talking about. Now we head this way a few hundred yards," he went on, suiting his actions to his words, "and we should come across a rock slide spilling off this ledge into the woods, and --"

Earl had caught up and was walking beside the ranger, when he let out a whoop. "Yow! There it is! First the ledge, and the rock slide, just like you expected. I'll be damned. Is this where the money is?"

"This is where we're going to search. At least, not quite here. First we skirt this slide, which points us back toward the road. It's pretty good-sized, and it should bring us fairly close to the road we were on but a little higher up." Warren was following his own instructions as he spoke, and before long they were indeed at the terminus of the slide.

Further exploration revealed the road only a short distance away. Selecting a point midway between the southerly side of the road and the end of the slide, Warren tapped his foot significantly. "This is where we hunt." He retrieved the scintillator and quickly assembled it, smiling briefly at Earl as he did so. "I'm getting pretty good at this. Practice."

"And I'm getting pretty good at lugging it around, too. Practice," Earl griped good-naturedly. Both men felt relieved at having reached their goal, and at having something to occupy their thoughts. "Speaking of which, since I packed it all this way I ought to get first crack at using it."

"Fine by me. Your scintillator, sir." Warren handed it over with a flourish.

After Earl fiddled with the knobs, the contraption produced the smooth humming sound they recognized from their previous experience with it. "Good," said Warren with pleasure. "Now run it over, umm, my watch to check it out."

Earl did so, and the machine's hum ascended into a squeal, signalling the presence of metal. "Good thing we left Jake behind. As I recall, he wasn't overly fond of that noise."

"Yeh." Warren chuckled but immediately became businesslike. "Let's start here. There's not much space between the slide and the road, and there shouldn't be any other metal here at all. No nails," he said with relief. "So it should go quickly."

Earl nodded and began swinging the disc of the scintillator over the ground in overlapping circles so as not to miss anything. The instrument hummed persistently, with Earl moving slowly and methodically. Back and forth, back and forth the disc swung. Warren settled himself into a sitting position on a conveniently broad rock, listening intently.

"Nothing in that swath, Warren, from road to rocks."

"Try shifting to the west a little and do the same thing, from road to rocks. Make sure you overlap with what you just did."

Obediently Earl moved his operations slightly and repeated the procedure, starting from the rocks and heading toward the road. About halfway there, the scintillator emitted a howl that brought Warren to his feet, and in two bounds to Earl. "That's it! You've got it! I'll get the shovel."

The ranger dashed back to the rucksack, grabbed the shovel, ran back and started digging furiously. As he dug, he spoke to Earl in snatches. "Not deep ... no shovel. Quick job, probably. Some pain."

"Save your breath for digging, Warren. You can explain it to me later. Right now I can't wait to lay eyes on that money." Earl laid the scintillator aside and fixed his gaze on the growing hole.

Taking Earl's advice, Warren concentrated on digging. In the excitement of the find he had forgotten to put on any gloves, and a rough spot on the shovel handle was biting into his palm, but he didn't take time to stop and don gloves. Only a few minutes later the shovel hit resistance and produced a solid-sounding thunk when Warren drove it down into the earth. The two men stared at each other for a second, then Warren redoubled his efforts. In no time the oblong lid of a steel box was revealed.

"You're a son of a gun, Warren," Earl stated. "How you figured this out I do not know, but by God you did it!"

"Let's not celebrate yet, Earl," Warren cautioned. "We'd better see what's in here before we uncork the champagne."

"What else could be in there but the money?" demanded Earl. "This isn't exactly where old boxes go to die. Get on with it! Here, let me spell you." Wresting the shovel away, Earl proceeded to enlarge the hole sufficiently to lift the box out. "Hey, how about a hand, Warren? This thing is heavy. Must be stuffed with money."

Squatting beside the hole and reaching down, Warren grasped one end of the box while Earl took the other. "No point in guessing when we can open it and find out. Just don't get your hopes up over that money, Earl."

Straining to extricate the strongbox from its grave, Earl uttered between grunts, "Why not? There's nothing else this could be."

"Actually, that's not quite so. If I'm right --"

"And so far you have been, Warren," said Earl grandly. "I won't quibble with that."

"Here, pull up on that corner there. It's hung up on something. If I'm right," the ranger continued, "there won't be any money in here."

Earl sat down with a thud as the box suddenly loosened. "Omph. Ow! No money? You're not looking for the money? You're looking for no money? We're up here not to find the money? You lost me, Warren."

Ignoring Earl's monologue, Warren eagerly turned the box around and eyed the rusty lock. "Won't take much to get rid of that," he observed. Holding the shovel upside down, he rammed the handle between the prongs of the padlock and pried against the metal with all his might. The lock gave one squawk as the metal gave way, then snapped and flew off. He leaned down and lifted the lid off.

24

Warren and Earl bumped heads over the box as they both leaned forward greedily. There was no sound for a moment, and then Earl half-shouted, "Butcher paper!" "Butcher paper," Warren echoed with obvious satisfaction. "Thank God for butcher paper." He stuck his hand and lifted up a batch of mouldering paper, then placed it gently back down as it began to disintegrate in his fingers. "Better not touch it. We need this just how we found it to get Monty out of this pickle."

Dropping back to his sitting position, Earl shook his head. "Mind drawing me a picture, Warren? Even I can figure out that somebody made a switch somewhere along the way, but who? Okay, we already know that these thieves were double- crossing each other, contrary to the popular opinion about honor among thieves, but which one of 'em could have made the substitution?"

Apparently lost in his own thoughts, Warren made no answer. Earl continued with his reflections.

"Not Pritchart, he never made it out of the bank. Presumably not the corpse at the mill, because then he'd be the one with the money and not have to chase down Monty for it. The only person who knew where ..." Earl jumped to his feet. "Warren! God Almighty, old Doc Golden is the --"

The sound of a gunshot interrupted Earl's contemplations. Both men froze as they tried to identify the direction from which the sound, distant but clear, had come. The noise bounced off the rock face behind them, mocking their attempts to locate its source.

"Hell's bells!" Warren said. "That better be just some poacher getting a jump on the season."

Another gunshot greeted this hope, followed by a volley. "If that's a hunter he found himself one wily buck -- it's shooting back," Earl observed drily.

"Let's go," Warren commanded. "If we don't make it in time, they'll be making venison out of Monty." And he sprinted up the slope, Earl close on his heels.

They loped on for some twenty minutes, stopping occasionally to take their bearings or listen when they heard firing. Finally Earl dropped to the ground, panting. "I gotta have a break, Warren. A track star I ain't." He stretched his legs out in front of him and pressed his arms against his stomach.

"Okay, Earl, you stay put. I mean to --" Warren interrupted himself and listened intently. He peered into the forest around him, then suddenly heard a quiet voice behind him.

"That'll do, gents. No sudden moves, hands up, don't do anything stupid."

Slowly Warren extended his arms up and turned around. A state police officer leaned carelessly against a tree, pointing a rifle in their direction. It was the same officer present at the shake mill when Alice had come to view the body.

"Well, well, what have we here?" the officer said smugly. "You two keep turning up like those old bad pennies. Or maybe it's not coincidence. Last time I saw you, you seemed mighty fond of Lewis. Maybe you're here to keep an appointment?"

"Come off it, you --" Earl was cut off by Warren.

"Officer, we have important evidence in this case. It proves Monty Lewis is innocent of the original robbery in Milford thirty years ago, and it explains this last killing, too. This manhunt has to be called off. Who's in charge of it?"

Grinning, the officer spit out a fir needle he had been chewing on. "I've gotta hand it to you, you don't give up easy. Sure, if you say so Mr. Ranger, I'll just run up and call off the hunt for a convicted murder and robber wanted for a second murder and on the lam, all because Ranger Rob says I should."

Warren swallowed this sarcasm without visible irritation. "I've got to get through to you. This is serious. Monty may be killed by those ... those buddies of yours up there, and he's an innocent man. If you don't want to do anything about it, then don't waste my time. I'll do it myself." Warren lowered his arms from their rather ridiculous posture in the air, and turned his back on the policeman.

"Warren!" Earl called, urgently but needlessly. The ranger had heard the officer's movement, heard the click as the rifle was cocked and the safety snapped off.

"I wouldn't recommend it," the state trooper said smoothly. "As far as I'm concerned, you're some kind of accessory here. After the fact at least, maybe before the fact, too. It also strikes me that you're involved in helping a known felon to escape a police search, another strike against you, and you're probably obstructing justice to boot. Anyway, we'll throw that in for good measure. You'd better think before you step, Ranger, because I'm justified in shooting you if you try to escape."

Warren turned back to face his adversary, who was now concentrating his full attention on the ranger, pointing the rifle directly at his chest. With no warning, a flying rock hit the trooper square in the head, and he dropped quietly to the ground, stunned. Amazed, Warren stared at Earl, who had now risen and was brushing off his hands in a business-like way. Taking in his friend's shocked face, Earl commented casually,

"I may not be a track star, but in my day I was one mean shot putter." He chuckled. "Well, I've had my rest. Shall we proceed?"

Warren laughed loudly. "Let's. And I personally will pay for the lawyer to defend you against a charge of assaulting a police officer."

"I'll hold you to that, too. Just don't get me Crook or Lynch, please. Fowl I could live with. Come on. That won't keep him down for long." They resumed their race through the woods.

Sounds other than shots were penetrating to them now. Shouted orders and responsive calls could be heard. Listening as they moved, Earl and Warren gained a better idea of the activity around them.

"They've spread out to cover more area," Earl suggested.

"Agreed. And they're heading uphill." Warren racked his brain to recall the topography ahead of them. "Wait a minute," he said, coming to a stop. "Let's think instead of running blindly. Where would Monty be heading?"

Puffing slightly, Earl said, "We'll be at the timberline soon, and so will the cops, although they probably don't know that. It's wide open above that, just the alpine meadow. No where to hide. Monty would know enough to avoid that, but they're heading straight for it."

"Good thinking. Monty will stay in the timber, but he probably wants to get over Coffin to avoid getting trapped on this side." " Seems to me the best we can do is stick to the timber for a while yet, then cut across the meadow where it's narrowest. That's probably how Monty would figure it." Without waiting to discuss it further, Earl took the lead and angled off from their original path in a line roughly parallel with the timber line above them. Warren followed.

Making every effort to move quietly but quickly, they jogged through the trees, the fir needles softening their footfalls. Nonetheless they didn't outpace the police, who had indeed reached the meadow and could move unhindered and seemingly in the same direction as Earl and Warren. Before long the woods around the two thinned noticeably, more sunlight reached them, and Earl came to a sudden halt.

"What is it?" Warren demanded in an undertone.

In answer, Earl simply pointed. Ahead of them, stretching as far as they could see in every direction, was a forest of skeletons: eerily-glistening trees, bare from any trace of leaf, needle or bark, yet intact in trunk and limb, strangely beautiful as they towered over their puny human observers. There were no boughs for the wind to sigh in here, and it passed through silently. Moss had grown up on the ground in place of the thick layer of fir needles behind them, tinting the earth a deep yet subtle green, in stark contrast to the silvery-grey of the trees. No squirrel chattered, no bird called.

"The ghost forest," Warren breathed.

Shattering the weird peace cast by the bleached trees, a bullet pierced the stillness, splintering a small branch into flying white fragments.

"Lewis is up above!" came a yell startlingly close to Warren and Earl. "Move out!"

Whispering in his friend's ear, Earl said, "This is our last chance to get to Monty before they do. In fact, before they get to us. Come on, we're a step ahead of them."

Pressing ahead through the otherworldly light from the sun reflecting off a thousand ghostly trees, the two headed upward cautiously but rapidly, listening to the noisy progress of the police nearby. Abruptly Warren stopped and held his arm out in front of Earl, who also halted. Signalling for silence, the ranger turned his head from side to side. Then Earl heard it, too. The hunters had divided up, and could be heard from above them as well as from below.

Indicating a new direction with a movement of his head, Warren altered their course and started moving again, more quickly this time. He had only covered a short distance, however, when with a stifled grunt he tripped and fell heavily on the ground. Glancing back, he saw the reason: the butt of a rifle extended out from behind a wide tree trunk. Seeing the obstruction, Earl circled the tree and exclaimed softly. Propped against the broad trunk was Monty Lewis, blood staining his shirt front and the ghostly white of the tree.

25

"Jesus, Monty!" Earl whispered, and knelt beside him.

Warren scrambled around the tree. "It's best if we all stay down," he said in a low voice. "Is he conscious?"

Hearing the question, Monty opened his eyes and nodded. "Just barely," he said weakly. "Too ornery to die." After a pause he added, "unless you're here to finish the job."

"No," responded Warren, as emphatically as he could in a whisper. "Alice asked us to find you, and we've been looking for days. Don't worry, we'll get you out of here."

With apparent effort Monty focussed his eyes on the ranger. "Warren? Alice told me when I saw her last. Jeez, was it today? Seems like ..."

Earl interrupted. "Save your breath, Monty. We'll thrash it all out later. Just sit tight." As he spoke he opened Monty's jacket and shirt and attempted to examine the wound. "Looks like you had sense enough to get the bleeding stopped, anyhow. Can't say that it looks good, though. Wish I knew whether the bullet was still in there. If it went clean through, we might risk moving him."

Shaking his head dolefully, Monty said breathlessly, "You'd have to pack me out. I can't take a step under my own steam."

"He's right," agreed Warren. "Too risky to move him. Too much blood loss. We'll just have to turn him in and let the cops get him out. Once they find he's been hit they'll calm down."

In his agitation at these words Monty shook his head emphatically, and uttered a soft groan at the movement. "No! These guys have already smelled blood in the water."

"I can't figure it out," Earl said quietly. "Granted, these guys are not exactly mental giants, but surely they wouldn't open fire for no reason."

"... reason," answered Monty in a whisper, "I clipped one of 'em. Didn't know ... cops here. After some venison, two days no meal."

"Hush now, Monty," Warren ordered softly. "Don't try to explain."

"Got to." Monty seemed to be fading fast. "Shoot to kill order. Heard it. They're to ..." he stopped to gather his strength, then continued. "... sound shoot. Hear sound, shoot, no questions."

In spite of himself, Warren glanced nervously around. He had heard of sound shooting, which struck him as very unsound, but hadn't seen it practiced before. Being in the immediate vicinity of the practice did not seem to be a very good policy. And without warning, he saw the sound shoot order carried out.

From somewhere in the depths of the ghost forest floated a wail, ghastly, shrill and unutterably terrified. It reverberated in the pale forest, its pathos and desperation ladening the light-filled air. Even while its notes were still ringing, the police rifles burst into action, peppering the woods in the general direction of the mysterious call. The silence that followed seemed even deeper after the explosion of sound.

The hunted trio huddled closer together. Warren shrugged his shoulders as if in answer to a unasked question.

Earl finally said, "I never heard such a caterwauling in my life. Somebody must have been murdered!" Warren gestured for silence, but Earl continued softly. "One thing's for sure, they're so damn edgy now they'll shoot at the drop of a feather. Listen up. I'll make my way uphill a ways, put some distance between me and you." He paused to check up on the police activity as they attempted to locate the source of the sound at which they had fired. "Once I've got a safe distance between us, I'll get behind a tree, or better yet find a fallen log and hunker down behind it, dig myself in under it a bit, and give a shout. Even if they fire I'll be covered, and I'll keep on shouting to explain who I am, that I'm not Monty, I'm not armed but I'll lead 'em to Monty if they'll give me half a chance. I'll offer to walk in front of 'em as they get close here so they won't feel like they have to blow Monty's head off to protect themselves."

"No chance, Earl. Are you forgetting that you crowned a policeman? He must have caught up to the rest by now and let them know about us. We're just as bad as Monty in their eyes -- worse, in fact, after hitting a cop. None of us would live to tell the tale." Warren carefully rearranged his lanky body and took off his jacket. "I have something else in mind." He proceeded to put Monty's buffalo-plaid cap on his own head and cover Monty with his jacket as if with a blanket; then, gently, with as little movement as possible, he removed the coat from the now-unconscious Monty and wore it himself. Earl eyed him with alarm.

"Warren, what are you up to?"

Squirming to fit into the coat, the ranger whispered back, "Crude but effective. The old decoy trick. You're a hunter. You must have used it yourself many a time. This'll get them out of the area. You stick right here, keep Monty as warm as you possibly can. If he comes to, give him some of that chocolate of yours. I'll be back as soon as I can, so don't move or I'll never find you."

"And you said my scheme was too dangerous! Look, Warren, you stay with Monty and I'll go."

"No good. I'm not exactly eager to do this, Earl, but there's more to it than getting out of here. Whoever goes has to get back again and bring help. I don't think Monty will make it through a night up here. We don't dare get help officially, but I have access to all the Forest Service equipment, including the firefighters' helicopters. I'll get Doc Golden and roust out a pilot from the barracks. We'll land right on top of Coffin Mountain, as close as we can. I think we can get within about a quarter of a mile from here. If I'm lucky, we'll have Monty in the hospital before dark, and the cops won't dare take a shot at him there."

Resigned, Earl nodded and gave the thumbs-up signal. He watched as the ranger disappeared from view, then removed his jacket, shirt and even his undershirt and spread them over Monty as best he could, hoping that the extra warmth would prevent the injured man from going into shock. Still not satisfied, Earl removed his trousers and used them as extra cover over Monty's legs and, sitting on the moss in only his shorts, socks and boots he tried to track Warren's progress by sound. For quite some time he heard nothing at all except Monty's shallow breathing. After what seemed an hour he heard an excited shout, a rifle shot and a general bustle of movement around him. The police moved out after their quarry, leaving Monty and Earl alone in the ghost forest.

***

Doc Golden jumped at the pounding on the back door. "Heavens to Betsey!" he exclaimed petulantly, with syringe in mid-air. "What in -- tarnation," he glanced at the ten-year old on his examining table, "can that be?"

"You better go find out, Doc," his patient advised energetically. "I can wait!"

"Hmph. I guess you'll have to." The doctor headed for the back. "Alright, alright. Keep your shirt on!" By the time he reached the back door his patient had escaped the examining room and rejoined his mother in the waiting area, informing her that the doctor was finished with him and they could go home.

Dr. Golden opened the door, prepared to read the riot act to somebody. "Warren! What --"

"Emergency, Doc. Grab your bag. You'll be a long way from civilization."

Not taking the time to ask a single question, the doctor did as he was bidden and reappeared immediately with his gear. "Let's go."

"Mind if we take your car, Doc?"

"Course not. Where to?" The doctor fished the car keys from his pocket, threw his bag in the back and climbed behind the wheel, not noticing Warren's wary look around on their way to the car.

"The ranger station, the barracks there."

Backing carefully out the driveway, the doctor threw a glance at his passenger. "Thought you said we'd be away from civilization. That's not so far."

"That's just the beginning. Hope you like helicopters." Suddenly Warren ducked down behind the dash board.

"Say! What are you playing at there, Warren?" Then the doctor noticed the police car approaching, and looked shrewdly at the top of Warren's head. "Tying your shoe, I suppose?" He lifted his hand in a friendly salute as they met the police cruiser, which was heading the opposite direction. Checking his rearview mirror repeatedly, he eventually said, "All clear. You can sit up now."

The ranger did so. "Thanks. Guess I owe you an explanation."

"I wouldn't be against one," Dr. Golden responded judiciously. "I also wouldn't mind knowing what kind of medical emergency I'll be up against."

"Gunshot wound." Warren gave the doctor a succinct account of the drama he had witnessed. "Quite a bit of blood loss, I think," he wound up, "and I don't know what else."

"Crazy troopers," his listener muttered. "S'pose I'll patch him up just so they can arrest him."

Firmly Warren stated, "Not if I have my way. I can prove, thanks to your dad, that Monty had nothing to do with it. All we have to do is keep Monty alive long enough to enjoy it."

"My dad? How do you figure him in the picture?" The doctor navigated the car up the narrow road to the barracks, and parked near the door. Again Warren ducked down.

"I'll tell you later about your dad. For all I know the police have a bulletin out on me, Doc. You better go in and find one of the helicopter pilots. Any one of 'em will do. Tell him there's a medical emergency you've been requested to see to up in the back country, and that the helicopter use has been authorized by the ranger district. If he wants to see the paperwork, tell him it's been sent on to the heliport and you'll show it to him there. I'll take your car and meet you there, you take one of the rigs from here."

"Right. See you at the heliport."

At the heliport Warren had to wait only a few minutes before the pilot and doctor arrived. After seeing which helicopter they entered, he grabbed the doctor's bag from the back seat and clambered in behind them.

"Mr. Ascott!" the pilot said with surprise. Warren recognized him as Rodney Malson, one of the few older men to make the grade as a chopper pilot. "Didn't know you'd be flying with us. Heard over the two-way radio that the police need to see you."

"I know it, Rodney. I need to see them, too, but first things first. I'm the only one who knows where this injured fellow is. The police'll have to wait."

Doubtfully Malson agreed. "Guess that makes sense. Where to?"

"Coffin Mountain. Land on the west end, it's flat there and it should be wide enough. This thing is equipped with a stretcher, isn't it?"

The pilot nodded. "Standard equipment. Emergency food supply, too, and a first-aid kit."

The rotors thundered to life above them, drowning conversation. Dr. Golden shouted to make himself heard. "How do you close the door?"

"No doors," the pilot shouted back.

"No doors?" The doctor turned and glared at Warren in the seat behind him, who lifted his shoulders in a gesture of helplessness, then leaned forward and strapped the doctor in with a seat belt. The helicopter soared up vertically, then banked and headed toward Coffin Mountain. Dr. Golden gasped as the chopper tilted during its banking, leaving only open air between him and the ground. Then it straightened, and he sat back and actually started enjoying the ride; but suddenly he recalled Monty lying bleeding on a mountain, and issued a heart-felt but silent prayer as he was carried into the heavens.

26

Earl stomped heavily around the tree in an effort to stop the shivers that made him tremble from head to foot. The sunshine was very thin at this elevation, and even that was fast disappearing. He had taken a bite from his chocolate bar, but resisted eating more in case Monty came to and could swallow some. After the initial relief of knowing the police had deserted the area, the unworldly calm of the forest had become somehow oppressive. Earl remembered vividly the scream that had rent the air earlier, and decided to stop his tramping in favor of standing near Monty with his back to the broad tree trunk.

At last the uneven beating of rotors, sounding like a huge banner flapping in wind, reached Earl's ears, and he eagerly scanned the sky. Softly at first, then louder, the noise came to him, and he lay his head against the tree and heaved a great sigh.

"Cavalry's here," he muttered to himself, and watched with elation as the chopper broke over the horizon of Coffin Mountain, hovered uncertainly for a moment, then descended awkwardly to the mountain's surface and out of Earl's view. He hastened to Monty's rifle, picked it up, cocked it and made himself as comfortable as he could for the last leg of his wait.

The whirring of the helicopter died away, and Earl felt momentarily abandoned. Then he chided himself and listened for other signs of activity. Before long his vigilance was rewarded with the sound of human voices, apparently shouted instructions of some kind. Pointing the rifle straight up, Earl fired a single shot. More calls back and forth followed this, and he fired a second time and, after an interval of a few minutes, a third. Finally human figures appeared between the boles of the silvery trees.

"Earl! If you can hear us, give us a holler!" Warren's voice floated down.

"Dead ahead! Keep coming!" Earl shouted jubilantly, and waved his arms.

Doc Golden peered into the deepening twilight. "I see something white moving up ahead." They pressed on. "It's Earl! Why're you so white? Oh, you're darn near stark naked!"

"You don't have to rub it in, Doc," Earl called out. "I happen to be aware of the fact."

Ignoring the chit-chat around him Warren, who was helping Malson carry a stretcher, went straight to Monty. Malson felt a thrill of alarm when he first spied the figure propped against the tree, and for a moment wondered whether the mountain they were on not only looked like a coffin, but had also become one, of a sort. The ranger's tense voice interrupted his speculations.

"Take a look, Doc. Can we move him?"

After a brief examination, the doctor replied. "You damn well better. There's nothing I can do here." He instructed the pilot and the ranger how to handle the inert body, and with the utmost gentleness spread a blanket over Monty's form on the stretcher. "Poor kid," he said quietly. Noticing the extra clothes already over the unconscious figure, he smiled gratefully at Earl. "Here, take my coat, Earl." He handed it over, and without another word they trooped up the mountainside and out of the woods.

* * *

The distinctive and unalterable hospital smell greeted Alice as she hurried through the lobby and into the elevators. Punching the button marked three, she held her finger firmly against it until the doors opened on the desired floor. The first sight she saw was Warren leaning against the corridor wall opposite the elevators. He smiled reassuringly as she ran out.

"He's doing fine, Alice," the ranger said as he gave her a quick hug. "He even regained consciousness for a few minutes, but he's out again now, which the doctor says is A-okay. They gave him some blood and now he just needs to rest."

"Oh, Warren, really?"

"You bet your boots, Alice."

After controlling herself through the many tension-filled days, at last Alice Lewis broke down and cried in Warren's arms. Eventually the sobbing subsided into sniffles, and she regained her composure.

"Can I see him?"

"You'll have to ask the doctor about that." Warren pointed out the attending physician and Alice hurried off. Smiling reflectively, Warren walked downstairs and to the main entrance where Earl was waiting for him.

"I heard the good news," he commented to the ranger.

"Yup. Where'd you get the pants?"

"Doc Golden took pity on me and retrieved mine from the stretcher. He wants to stay for awhile and give advice to the doctors here. Guess he's pretty fond of Alice and Monty -- I couldn't pry him away from this hospital tonight. But at least you and I can call it a day. I phoned for my wife to come get us. She should be here pretty soon. Thank God this whole escapade is over."

Frowning, Warren replied, "It's not over yet, Earl. We still have a long row to hoe."

"Meaning what?"

"Meaning, the cops still haven't got the foggiest idea what's been going on. Monty's out of their clutches for the moment, but I still have to persuade them that he's not their man."

"Come to think of it, you still have to explain that to me, too."

Slapping Earl on the shoulder, Warren said, "That would suit me to a tee, buddy, but I think this outfit is going to demand first service." He looked out through the glass doors at the state police car that had just pulled up and was disgorging what seemed like an infinite number of troopers. "This might take a while." And Ranger Ascott sat down calmly on a well-worn sofa in the waiting room.

"At least tell me one thing, Warren. Who masterminded Monty's kidnapping and killed Barney Pritchart?"

"Oh, that," said Warren absently. "I thought you must have guessed by now. It was Gil Callahan." Just then the troopers, entering the lobby, caught sight of the two men and swarmed around them.

27

Laughter echoed through the old mansion as Monty and Alice's grandchildren rollicked through the hallways, up and down the stairs, and occasionally erupted into the rooms. At one point Josh Lewis' booming voice commanded:

"If you kids want to rough-house, go on outside in the yard and do it, not in here where you might break something of Grandma and Grandpa's."

Monty Lewis stretched happily on the sofa. "Now, son, don't be too hard on 'em. That's a damned fine sound they're making if you ask me. I didn't see hide nor hair of a kid in a good many years. Let 'em be."

"Oh, Dad," Mary said, bending down to kiss Monty on the forehead, "you're going to have a hard time getting rid of them from now on. All they ask for these days is Grandpa, Grandpa, Grandpa. You're better than a new toy," she concluded with another kiss.

Alice Lewis, glowing as Warren had never seen her before, scurried happily between her children, grandchildren and other guests, but was never away from Monty for more than a few moments at a time. "The ice cream is almost ready," she announced. "Who wants to lick the beaters?" This caused a general exodus of persons under the age of twelve, leaving the grown-ups to return to their favorite topic.

"Out with it, Warren," Earl Millican demanded. "The doc and I have been sitting here long enough trying to get the whole picture, but we give up."

"That's right," the doctor concurred. "What's really got me fit to be tied is how my father got mixed up in this. You said he's the one who led you to the strongbox. How come?"

Helping himself to another huckleberry muffin, Warren explained. "That report he filed on Gil Callahan's death did it. Hold on, I guess I better backtrack some first."

"Please! I don't get why you were interested in that to begin with," interjected Josh. "You and dad seem to have the whole thing pegged out. Were you in touch with each other?"

"No way!" Monty spoke up. "I just learned a few things talking to Tony Ansca. Man alive, did I get a turn when I saw him in Salem! It was like seeing myself in a ... well, not exactly a mirror. He wasn't my perfect double, but boy he was close enough to be an old photograph of me. But he didn't know much. I coulda dug from here to Christmas without getting to the bottom of it. In fact, I had no idea there was anybody else in my court -- it gave me quite a boost when Alice told me you guys were trying to clear me." He included both Warren and Earl in his appreciation. "Kept me going to an amazing extent up there in the woods after I took off, just knowing I wasn't the only one who knew I was innocent."

With gentle reproof Alice said, "You were never the only one, Honey." Perching on the arm of the sofa near his head, she put her hand in his.

"Well, besides you, Alice." He lifted her hand and touched it to his cheek. "Actually, there is nobody besides you." He kissed her hand.

They were interrupted by the chattering grandchildren. "Can we go play in the attic, Mom? It's really neat up there."

Alice answered for Mary. "Neat? Not by a long shot. It's dusty and cobwebby."

"That's what we mean. It's neat! And there's that great big metal thingamajig."

Answering her daughter's questioning glance, Alice said, "The rainwater cistern. I've been using it alot this last year. Okay, you can play up there. Be careful on the stairs." With a general whoop the siblings and cousins ran joyfully out of the room.

"Tony Ansca," said Doc Golden with some impatience. "He's the one they found out at the mill, I take it. How did he meet his maker, anyhow?"

"Accident," said Monty brusquely.

"In a pig's eye! I saw that wound to his head," interposed the doctor. "He wasn't hit once, he was hit several times, and with great force."

Agreeably, Warren said, "That's a fact. But it was still an accident. Right, Monty?" Not waiting for an answer, Warren went on. "You saw only his head, Doc. The state cops actually did one thing right. They had a thorough post-mortem done, which showed bruises and lacerations on his back and legs. As if," here he glanced at Earl, "he'd been caught in an avalanche."

"Avalanche? Not that rock slide where you found the strong box?"

"Nope," Warren negated this. "Not a natural avalanche. My guess is he got trapped under a slew of mill debris, probably right at the shake mill where he was found. That must be where you caught up to him, Monty, am I right?"

"Hold on here." Mary complained, "Can't you guys start at the beginning? I can't make head or tails of what you're talking about."

This sentiment was echoed en masse. Warren thought for a moment, then began anew.

"The beginning is one long time ago. Back in 1934, in fact. Roosevelt was president. The Sears, Roebuck catalogue was everybody's wishbook. Jobs were few and far between, but your folks, Mary and

Josh," he glanced at their attentive faces and smiled, "were getting by."

Smiling fondly at his parents, Josh said, "I remember your canned venison, Mom."

"And the mink muff you got for your birthday!" Mary added. "The winters were so much colder back then, or does it just seem that way because I was little?"

"No, sweetheart," Monty assured her. "They really were colder, and with a heck of a lot more snow than we get nowadays. Sorry, Warren," he added. "We're all ears for your story. It's just hard to resist reminiscing a little."

Warren smiled. "Fine with me. Anyway, not everybody was doing as well as the Lewises. Tobe Tobias, for example, was on the verge of going under, in spite of his seeming prosperity. He had a good lumber business going, but the bottom had dropped out of the housing market. Nobody could afford even to remodel a place, let alone build a new one. But Tobe was a mean son of a bee; he wouldn't go down alone. Gil Callahan would go with him."

"We heard from Earl that Callahan was at the bottom of it," Dr. Golden stated. "But what's his connection?"

"I'm getting to that. Gil was out to make his fortune in this neck of the woods by building that railroad up the canyon, connecting the back country with the rail systems and big lumber markets to the east. Of course, that was a long- term project, which was started well before the depression hit. It was child's play to find investors for a scheme like that before the stock market crash of '29. Funny thing was, good old Gil kept going through their money without having many miles of rails to show for it. Before long he was clean through the first batch of invested money, and was hurting for more."

Thoughtfully, the doctor commented, "I remember my father talking about that. If my memory serves me correctly, he said that crook Tobias was squeezing Callahan for all he was worth. Let me see ... Running the biggest timber outfit around here the way he did, Tobe was a major prospective customer, and Gil got him in on the project from the start. In fact, Tobe was really the moving force in it, and he just contracted out the work to Callahan. Then, when Gil got hit by increasing construction costs, he couldn't make ends meet and Tobe really stuck it to him."

"Yes and no," replied the ranger. "Tobe was a sharp operator alright, to put it mildly. But Gil was no babe in the woods, so to speak." He turned to Monty. "Did you find out anything about him in San Francisco?"

Nodding emphatically, Monty answered, "And how! Probably the same things you found out there. He had a record a mile long before he hit Milford: fraud and embezzlement, mainly."

"Wait a sec, Warren," Mary interpolated. "What made you check up on Gil in the first place? I mean, why select him out of all the others to track down?"

"A couple things put me on to him. First of all, I figured that whoever robbed the bank wouldn't just hang around Milford or Haven for too long. After all, there's no point in robbing a bank if you're not going to enjoy the fruit of your labor; but any big change in a person's style of living would have been noticed here, and might have started somebody wondering where so-and-so got the money for a new car, or a bigger house, or what have you. So with the help of Miss Gustavson, the Milford town clerk, I nosed around in the records for somebody who left town not immediately, but some time after the robbery. That's when I noticed Callahan missing from the tax lists as of 1935, but I almost passed him by when Miss Gustavson came up with his death certificate to account for it." Warren paused to enjoy the apple cider Alice had set out.

Refilling his glass, she said, "Must be thirsty work. Drink up. There's lots more where that came from."

Mary took advantage of the interruption to run upstairs and check on the children. The sound of an engine out front sent Josh to the front door. "It's Sheriff Grinder," he announced. "Guess his curiosity got the better of him."

"You're darned tootin' it did," the sheriff admitted as he came up the walk. "Hello, Jake. Working like a dog, as usual, I see." He reached down and gave the dog, who was stretched luxuriously out in the sunshine, a quick pat on the head.

"Join the crowd, Sheriff," Monty called hospitably. "We won't let Warren stop and fill you in on what you've missed so far, but you can hear the grand finale anyway."

"And have some muffins and cider, too," offered Mary.

"Best offer I've had all day," said the sheriff, and made himself comfortable in an easy chair. "Don't let me stop you, Warren."

28

Recommencing his tale, Warren said, "Back to Gil Callahan, then. Since he seemed to be the only one to fit the bill as far as some connection with the bank (remember, there was alot of talk about his sizable deposits there), and nobody else seemed to have dropped out of sight, I figured it was worthwhile fleshing out the information on the death certificate, which was sketchy to say the least. No offense against your dad, Doc."

"None taken. I know what you mean about those old death certificates. Nine times out of time they stick in "heart failure" as the cause of death, without bothering to explain whether it was brought about by pneumonia, a heart attack, or a knife in the ribs."

"Exactly. So as most of you know, I prevailed on the doctor here to open up his old files. Including on you, Monty."

Turning his gaze rather reluctantly from his wife's face, Monty said, "My medical records? What for?"

Alice responded. "I didn't have time to tell you when you were here the other day, Monty. Warren and Earl found your gold tooth up on Coffin Mountain. They found the shack where you had been held, and the tooth there proved you had been there. I think," she added softly, "that's when they first started believing in your innocence."

Exchanging glances, Earl and Warren both started affirming their trust in Monty.

"Not so! We knew all along you couldn't have done it," Warren remonstrated. "We knew you were a straight shooter. Er, make that a straight arrow."

"A prince of a fella," Earl agreed.

"Downright upright," Warren wound up.

Grinning, Monty put in, "Enough already! Like I'd blame you for having some doubts. Who wouldn't? Except my Alice, of course."

"Anyhow," the ranger said, "we were proceeding on the assumption that you hadn't been involved in the robbery, Monty, so we were looking at it from a different angle than the investigators had in '34. So when I checked out the doctor's report on Gil, I found out that the body had been found up toward Coffin, right near a then-recent rock slide. Your father, Doc, was astute enough to smell a rat in Gil's death, but couldn't tell anything definite. All he knew was that the body was found in an out-of-the-way spot, with a broken leg. Heart failure was the immediate cause of death, but it was noted that exposure to the elements apparently brought it on."

Dr. Golden, Jr. observed, "In other words, he froze to death. Probably what we'd call hypothermia now. With a broken leg he couldn't get far. How'd that happen? The broken leg, I mean."

"You might say he was killed by bad timing. That leg must have got broken in the original rock slide. The remains of the slide are still there; Earl and I saw them the other day. There was probably some blasting done nearby not long before, to get those logging roads in. Those trees, big as they are, can grow practically on bedrock, and did. Even a bulldozer will tip over if the surface isn't level enough, so they must have used dynamite to even it up a bit. That must have weakened the cliff that runs parallel to that old road, and what with the cold setting in and other natural changes, part of the cliff face gave way. It happens quite a bit in these parts, but usually there's nobody around to care. Gil was in the right place at the wrong time, taking that road to get over Coffin Mountain and out of the area."

Speculatively, Earl stated, "That's when he buried the strongbox, then. Presumably his horse took off when the rocks started flying. Gil fell and broke his leg, or got hit by a rock, but managed to hang on to that box. Knowing he couldn't get far in any case, and not wanting to get caught with that, he buried it. But say, Warren," he said plaintively, "that still doesn't explain why there was only butcher paper in the box. What happened to the money, and why would Gil bother to bury paper?"

"Ah, there you've hit the nail on the head, Earl," the ranger responded. "You probably assumed the bank robbery was attempted in order to steal money."

"Silly me," commented Earl sarcastically. "I should have known it was really to steal butcher paper."

Chuckling, Warren said, "Not exactly. It was staged to steal the strongbox which Gil knew was already full of nothing but paper. In other words, Callahan arranged the whole robbery to cover up the fact that the strongbox he had left in the bank with such fanfare, supposedly stuffed with money from his investors, was nothing but a farce. He had already made off with that money, and socked it away in a bank in San Francisco. That's why he placed a locked box in the bank vault, instead of making a regular deposit, like you would expect a businessman to do. That way, no one would know he didn't deposit one thin dime of that money he had received."

Several people spoke at once on hearing this.

"You mean there never was any money stolen?"

"And people hunting for it for years!"

"The reward the investors put up for it!"

The babble continued for a few minutes, and then the ranger resumed his narrative.

"Not one penny did Gil deposit there. But he knew that sooner or later there'd be an audit, or a demand from his investors, or some damned thing that would foul up the whole game. So he planned a false robbery. And plan he did! First he got Pritchart, a questionable character to begin with, in on it because of Pritchart's knowledge of the bank. The inducement was a share of the loot, Pritchart of course having no way of knowing there was no loot to be shared. But Gil was still looking for another partner in crime, since he had already planned that Pritchart wouldn't make it out of the bank alive. When he went to San Francisco to salt away some more "investments" he came across Tony Ansca, a long-time hood and acquaintance of a fellow embezzler Gil knew in Frisco. The second he saw Ansca, Gil was put in mind of Monty Lewis. The resemblance in build and mannerisms really was striking, especially when Ansca faked a limp like Monty had; and with a scarf over a good part of his face, anybody could mistake him for Monty."

In a grim voice Alice exclaimed, "So that's why Gil maneuvered that clerk's job for Monty!"

Monty echoed her. "That's it, sure enough. And I thought it was because I was a good worker! The perfect patsy, more like it," he said bitterly.

"That's news to me," Warren said, to change the subject. "I didn't know Gil had his hand in that, but it makes sense. What really got me suspicious of Callahan was my talk with Gabe Hanks, the second talk, that is. He put me on the inside track on the dynamiting of the boardinghouse. Come to find out, Gil was the one who first suggested it."

"Yeah," Monty confirmed. "But what's the boardinghouse thing got to do with this?" he hurried to ask.

Judging rightly that Monty's guilty conscience about that incident had deflected his brooding on why he had been hired at the bank, Warren explained.

"Abner Brillo used that boardinghouse to store some of the bank records and what-not, including some of Callahan's records on how he supposedly spent the money of some of his previous investors. He knew those records of phony purchases and other expenditures wouldn't hold water if they were ever compared to his actual work on the railroad, and he had planned to steal them, too, during the robbery. But when he found out that Abner had transferred them to the boardinghouse, he had to take care of them a different way. So he blew it up. Simple and effective." The ranger carefully omitted any reference to Monty's part in the misadventure, but he could tell from Alice's troubled face that she was recalling it all too acutely.

"Then Tony Ansca was being used by Callahan, too, and promised part of the money from the robbery. Or did Callahan let him in on the real plan?" Dr. Golden suggested.

"Right the first time, Doc. Ansca was expecting a good-sized payment, I don't know exactly how much. Gil was planning to double-cross both his partners from square one, killing Pritchart during the robbery and leaving Ansca up at the shack to release Monty at the proper time. Incidentally, it was Gil's criminal record that led him to frame somebody. After spotting Ansca in Frisco, Monty was the clear choice here for a frame-up. Gil had to have a suspect so obvious that the police would go straight after him without investigating anybody else; Gil's background couldn't stand even the slightest scrutiny. It had taken him quite a few years to build his image as the legitimate man of business, and he wanted to preserve that so he could

171

eventually move elsewhere with his riches and have nobody on his trail. He'd gotten to enjoy being a solid, respected citizen."

At this point Mary posed a question. "All the same, Warren, why would this Ansca character leave Callahan behind with the money? Surely he didn't trust him that much."

"He didn't trust Gil one bit," Monty interjected. "That I know from my little chat with him recently. But he figured Gil wouldn't high-tail it with the money because Gil still needed Tony to handle me properly; Ansca had made it clear to Gil that if anything went wrong, he'd just 'find' me, back up my story and get Gil blamed for the whole kit and kaboodle. But when Gil did in fact disappear Ansca, who was not chosen for his brains, got hold of the wrong end of the stick. He got it in his thick head that Gil and I had cooked up a scheme to freeze him out. By then, though, the search for me had started, and with him looking so much like me he got nervous about being seen and have somebody put two and two together. He panicked and took off."

Sheriff Grinder put in his two cents worth on hearing this. "That's why he turned up in Milford last week! He was still convinced you knew where the money was, and when you got out of prison he came after you."

Monty verified that. "He knew by then that Callahan was dead, but he still stuck to his notion that I had been in on it with Gil, and he was bound and determined to get that money. What's more, over the years he had come to the conclusion that Callahan and I had plotted all along to turn on him, you know, the two local men getting together with the same story and pinning it all on the out-of-town con. Ansca figured that Callahan's death, which he somehow knew about, was the only thing that stopped us from doing that, and that I now had the money all to myself."

A pause followed, as those present digested all the information they had heard. Finally Dr. Golden repeated his earlier query. "So what did happen to Ansca? How did he die?"

"Well," Monty said, "Warren seemed to have that pretty well scoped out. I followed Ansca around until I could catch him in an out-of-the-way spot. I didn't want us to be interrupted," he added grimly. "From what I've heard here today, I guess he was retracing Callahan's steps of thirty years ago. Anyhow, he was holed up out at the old mill there, a pretty good spot, really -- isolated yet sheltered. That's where we had our little talk, and from his ranting I gathered what I just told you about him. He was pretty worked up, and I figured I didn't have much chance of getting out of there alive. I was careful enough to wait until he had gone out back of the mill, under the old scrap-burner there, to do his business so that he wouldn't have his gun with him, or so I thought. We talked for a while, edgy, you know, both trying to get information from the other. When I'd had enough and started to take off, he was quick enough to get a shot off, but just a warning shot in the air to convince me he was serious. But that shot set off some kind of vibration in the old, rusty scrap bin above him, or maybe he sliced a cable or something. Anyway, the whole mess came down with a crash."

"And killed him?" Alice asked quietly.

"Not right off the bat. At least, I wasn't sure whether he was dead or just out. I packed him clear back to the mill and was going to take him farther, in hopes of getting him some help, but by the time we got inside the mill I knew there was no point. Then I heard a car pull up outside, and I didn't waste any time getting out of there."

29

The silence that ensued was broken by a subdued chuckle from Sheriff Grinder.

"What's funny, Ron?" asked Josh.

"I was just thinking of those state cops out behind the mill, picking up hundreds of pieces of mill scrap. That did my heart good."

"Why on earth?"

Responding to Mary's question, the sheriff said, "My men and I recovered the strong box from where Warren and Earl had left it ..."

"Speaking of which," interrupted Earl, "looks like I'm going to get out of that little episode of stoning a state trooper none the worse for wear. My lawyer --"

"That would be Attorney Fowl, I take it," Warren put in.

"Correct. He says that since I was acting in order to prevent a greater wrong than the one I committed," here he looked meaningfully at Monty, "then my little exercise in shot putting was justified and I won't be prosecuted for it."

A small ripple of applause met this statement, and Earl bowed ostentatiously. "Thank you, thank you. But I still can't figure out one thing. When we were up there in the ghost forest, after we found Monty ..." He trailed off.

"I know what's on your mind," said Warren. "That scream we heard! I've been trying to figure that out myself, but it's beyond me. Talk about creepy, though."

Monty spoke up. "High-pitched, eerie, mournful?"

"In spades!" affirmed Earl. "The weirdest thing I ever heard. Don't tell me you know what it is."

Laughing heartily, Monty responded. "You two give new meaning to 'babes in the woods.' Haven't you ever heard a cougar scream before?"

"Cougar my foot! Wounded buffalo maybe, but that was no cat!" said Earl heatedly.

Still grinning, Monty said, "You guys take the cake. What you heard was the death cry of a cougar, probably the very same damned one I was shooting at when the cops winged me. I had that in my sights as dinner -- I had totally given up on anything as tasty as a deer, and was too durned hungry to be picky -- but I guess my trigger finger isn't as steady as used to be. Must have been hit by a stray bullet in all the commotion, and kept quite until the moment of death. That's the way they do it."

Reluctantly, Warren admitted the possibility. "But I can't believe that unearthly sound came out of a cat."

"You got to get out in the woods more, Ranger," Monty advised.

"As I was saying," Sheriff Grinder resumed, as if no one had changed the subject, "once the cops saw the box full of paper, and heard Warren's story, and got in touch with the authorities in San Francisco to confirm Callahan's record, they were pretty much forced to at least check out Monty's claim that Ansca was killed by falling scrap. They finally found at least one piece with human blood and hair on it, in a pattern consistent with Monty's description of the whole thing."

In a soft voice Alice commented, "I'll bet that call you made from here last night didn't do any harm, either, Warren. I couldn't help but overhear. Well, actually, I eavesdropped when I heard you talking about Monty."

"I thought it couldn't hurt to call in a few favors. It just so happens the Forest Service nailed an arsonist in the national forest after the state cops had let him slip through their fingers. He was a very nasty fellow. We saved them a lot of embarrassment, not to mention manpower, so I called the second-in-command at the state headquarters. Just a lucky break that he owed me one. Anyway, he sent quite a contingent up there to the scrap pile. They're also officially reopening the Milford bank robbery case in spite of Monty's conviction. I'm only sorry it wasn't done right thirty years ago."

"We're not looking back," Alice said firmly, squeezing Monty's hand.

"Alice is right," Monty agreed. "Now that I finally know what happened to me ... to us," he amended, "I can finally put those ghosts to rest."

Laughing, Alice said, "Now that you mention ghosts, Honey, did you know we live in a haunted house?"

"Run that one by me again, would you?" Mary demanded.

"Warren probably knows more about it than I do, but apparently --"

Her account was interrupted by a loud thump from upstairs, followed by a childish howl and general hubbub. Mary was halfway out of the room before anyone else was even moving, but they all followed her quickly up the steps and into the attic.

"You started it!"

"I did not! You did it. Mommy, he's the one --"

"That's enough," Mary snapped with her utmost parental authority. "If you can't play up here peacefully, you won't play up here at all. It's very simple."

Anxiously Josh inquired, "Everything okay here?"

"Fine," Mary assured her brother. "The kids just got a little rambunctious, but that's over now." She gazed sternly at the children as she said it.

Dr. Golden pushed his way forward. "You do have a doctor in the house, you know."

"Thanks, Doc," said Mary, "but it's just a scraped knee. "I'll take him down and put some first-aid cream on it."

They headed back downstairs, with the rest of the group trailing behind. Only the doctor remained in the attic, staring with fascination at the cistern used to collect rainwater for household use. He circled around it a few times, tapped on it, scraped at it, and struck it with an iron rod he found tucked away in a corner. At last he descended and joined the others, who had picked up the topic of the Crossburn Curse again. As he entered the room, Warren was elaborating on the toll the curse had taken on those who occupied the house they were now in.

"Insanity, too," Warren stated. "Either they all died young, or lived to a ripe old insanity."

Monty remarked, "The last time I saw Art Crossburn was when I bought that Model T Ford from him. Remember that, Alice? He did look bad, all shaky and grey and years older than he was."

"And he didn't live much longer," Alice observed.

In a heavy, loud voice, Dr. Golden intoned, "I'm not surprised."

Startled by his demeanor, Alice queried, "What do you mean?"

"I mean, I think I found the source of the Crossburn Curse, and if you don't do something about it, it'll be the Lewis curse quick enough, too."

Monty shifted on the sofa so he could see the doctor, who was standing in the door. "Out with it, Doc. What's on your mind?"

"That cistern of yours up in the attic. You've been using it?"

Alice nodded mutely.

"Well, don't. It's made of lead."

Pensively, Warren said, "Lead. As in pencils?"

"As in lead poisoning," Dr. Golden said gruffly. "Every time you drink water from there, you ingest lead. May even get it through the skin when you wash with it, I'm not sure about that. I'm no toxicologist. But I do know that once lead gets in your system, it stays for a while. Attacks the bone marrow, for one thing, hurts the blood, causes anemia, maybe brain damage, even death."

"My God," Alice whispered. "The children! Shouldn't we --"

"Don't jump the gun, Alice," the doctor responded. "It takes long-term exposure to do the things I'm talking about. They just show up for a visit now and then, they'll be okay. You folks will, too, as long as you quit using the damn thing. Drill a well, tap a spring, just seal up that blamed cistern."

This revelation had them all chattering excitedly until the sound of a knock on the front door. Alice greeted the visitor hospitably although with some reserve.

"Hello. Can I help you?"

"Yes," responded the pretty young lady on the porch. "Mr. Ascott asked me to stop by. I hope you don't mind. I'm Miss Gustavson, the town clerk in Milford."

"Mind! We're happy to have you -- the more the merrier. Warren was telling us how you helped my Monty by digging up some old records. We're very grateful to you." Alice escorted her inside, where Warren greeted her warmly.

"I figured you wouldn't mind, Alice, if I invited one more."

"Not in the least. I was just thanking her for her help to Monty and me." Alice made introductions.

Miss Gustavson sat demurely and accepted some refreshment. Warren moved his chair beside hers and announced, "Perfect timing, Miss Gustavson. You will be thrilled to hear that we, that is Dr. Golden, have, I mean has -- the point is, we know what caused the Crossburn Curse!" he finished dramatically.

"You'd better repeat yourself, Mr. Ascott. I must have misunderstood you."

Warren looked at her mischievously. "I, Miss Gustavson," he said grandly, "do not chew my cabbage twice."

For ordering and information,
please contact:
Niagara Publications
35960 N. Santiam Highway
Gates, OR 97346
Phone (503) 897-2675

$6.95

plus $1.50 shipping and handling

Also by David and Lisa Barnhardt
and available from Niagara Publications:

Axidental Murder
(A Warren Ascott Mystery)

$4.95
plus $1.50 shipping and handling